Seasons in the Fields

Stories of a Golden West

John D. Nesbitt

Books by John D. Nesbitt

For the Norden Boys
Lonesome Range
Black Hat Butte
Red Wind Crossing
Rancho Alegre
Raven Springs
Coyote Trail
Black Diamond Rendezvous
Man from Wolf River
Not a Rustler
West of Rock River
North of Cheyenne
Poacher's Moon
Adventures of the Ramrod Rider
A Good Man to Have in Camp
Keep the Wind in Your Face
Shadows on the Plain
Field Work
Blue Horse Mesa: Western Stories
Antelope Sky: Stories of the Modern West
Seasons in the Fields: Stories of a Golden West

Two Novellas:
"Dead for the Last Time"
"Trouble in the Labor Camp"

Seasons in the Fields

Stories of a Golden West

John D. Nesbitt

SPEAKING VOLUMES, LLC
NAPLES, FLORIDA
2017

Seasons in the Fields

ISBN 978-1-62815-699-7

*For Steve Jacobs, classmate and friend of my
younger days, who encouraged me
to write stories such as these.*

Acknowledgments

"Daddy and Norma Jean" appeared in *Wyoming Writing 1987*; reprinted in *Owen Wister Review*, Fall 1988.

"Like a Cat Full of Ham" appeared in *West Wind Review*, Spring 1987.

"Peach Picking" appeared in *Boar's Tusk*, Vol. 2, 1986.

"Gunfight at Mesquite Creek" appeared in *Carolina Quarterly*, Spring/Summer 1979.

"Chicken on Sunday" appeared in *Wyoming Writing 1985*.

"Fat Winter" appeared in *West Wind Review*, Spring 1990.

"Linda Morena" appeared in *West Wind Review*, 1991.

"Shining in the Spring" appeared in *Hard Row to Hoe*, Summer 1991.

"Bachelor Trove" appeared in *Wyoming Writing 1994*; reprinted in *Chiricú*, 1994.

Five of these stories have won awards with *Carolina Quarterly*, *Owen Wister Review*, Wyoming Writers, and the Wyoming Arts Council.

To the editors and judges of the above publications and organizations, I would like to express my appreciation for their recognizing and encouraging my work.

Table of Contents

Daddy and Norma Jean

The fog had rolled in while I slept, so I awoke to a chilly damp morning. Moisture had beaded velvet-fine on the windows of the car, inside and out, and the blankets I slept under were limp, damp on the outside. When I first awoke, I thought I was still at the berry field, where we had slept in the car for a month.

After a moment, I realized I was alone. I remembered the night before. I was in a deep sleep when my dad woke me and asked me to go sleep in the car. Over the iron railing of the foot of the bed, I saw a very pretty Mexican lady. My dad walked with me out to the station wagon, where he had already let down the seat and rolled out the bedding. I crawled right in and locked the doors, like he told me to.

The morning was clammy outside, but I had to pee, so I put on my clothes and trundled out to water some geraniums. I remembered an incident a few days before, in the field where we picked green beans. I had been picking on my row, about two feet up from the ground, and I came to a place where the vines were wet. This had been in the afternoon when the vines were dry, and I realized that one of the braceros had had his little joke with the young gringo. I wouldn't have minded returning the joke now.

Back in the car, I sat in the front seat. I was glad we didn't have to go to work. The next field we were to pick had to wait an extra day, for the beans to size up. That was why we had a Monday off, and that was why my dad had gone to the bar on Sunday night. As I laced up my tennis shoes, I wondered what the day would bring. It wasn't off to a very good start. I tried the transistor radio, but it was as dead as it had been the night before, when I sat outside and tried to tune in the game. That had been disappointing—I didn't know who was supposed to pitch, but it might have been Koufax. He was having trouble with his pitching hand and might be out for the rest of the season, but if he was back in the line-up, I didn't want to miss him. He was liable to throw a no-hitter any time he went out.

Sitting alone in the cabin court was still better than the berry field,, where we had camped out of our old Ford station wagon for a month. Since I wasn't sixteen yet—wouldn't be until the end of September—I couldn't work on an orchard ladder, so my dad and I spent the first half of the summer doing the lighter labor of picking berries—blackberries, boysenberries, raspberries, loganberries, and sometimes currants. It was pretty clean work as well—not dirty and sticky like some fruit picking—and the Watsonville weather was cool. So we didn't need a bath except once a week, when we would come to town for a room, sometimes in an old hotel for two or three dollars, and sometimes at this same place.

My dad came out of the cabin, smoking a cigarette and wearing his straw cowboy hat. When he got in and sat behind the steering wheel, I noticed he was freshly shaven. He tried to be cheerful with me.

"Sleep O.K.?"

"Oh yeah," I said. "It was O.K." Actually, I had slept all right. It was just the waking up that got me.

"Gettin' hungry?"

"Yeah, kind of."

"My—uh—lady friend will probably stick around for a couple more hours."

"What time is it now?"

"Eight-thirty."

"You're not hungry, Dad?"

"Not really. Do you have any money, Jim?"

"I have about three dollars."

"What would you think of going and getting your breakfast, then? You can handle that, can't you?"

"Sure. I can go to the place we went before, the place with the blueberry syrup."

"Sounds like a good plan." He drew on his cigarette. "Of course, if you want to, you can come in and meet my friend. If you wanted." He ashed his cigarette.

"I think I'd rather go eat."

"Nice to have a day off, huh?"

"Yeah, it's O.K."

"What's the matter, son?" I must have sounded mopy to him.

"Oh, nothing. It's just that the radio battery was dead, and I didn't get to hear the game."

"Aw, hell," he said. "Too bad you missed it. You can get a newspaper and read up on it when you eat breakfast, can't you?"

"Probably."

He put out his cigarette in the ashtray and moved his left hand up to the door handle. I noticed he still had the room key in his hand. He paused, trying, it seemed, not to be in a hurry. "You don't mind, do you?"

"No, I understand."

"That's a good sport. Enjoy your breakfast."

As I walked along through town, I thought about how far we had come already this summer. When we first hit the road, we had lived cheap. We had to. We didn't find work at first, so we ate cold food. Some of it, like the canned macaroni and pork and beans, we had with us. The rest of it we pinched out of our meager finances—sardines and crackers, white bread and baloney, Velveeta cheese that to this day still makes me gag. When I pulled our last twenty-dollar bill from my sock (I learned to wear the bill on top of my foot, on my instep), my dad said, "I sure as hell hope we find something pretty soon."

I did too. I didn't mind going without candy, and I didn't mind my father having to roll his own cigarettes. But I didn't like having to sleep behind service stations, and I really disliked my morning chore of taking the thermos bottle into a cafe and asking to have it filled with hot water. I must have looked dismal, because the waitresses treated me with sympathy and never charged me. My dad was good about letting me pick the cafe so I wouldn't go to the same one two days in a row. That was when I started drinking coffee, when I was grown-up enough to beg the hot water for it.

When we found work, it was only berry picking, which paid about eight dollars a day each. It wasn't much, but we managed to buy a camp stove. Life at the edge of the berry field became better, taking in luxuries like fried Spam or heated canned spaghetti, plus a room in town on Saturday. From there we went to picking green beans at two-and-a-half cents a pound, which came to a little better than ten dollars a day. That got us a room for $17.50 a week, and already I didn't care to look back. For that reason, I think, I awoke with an empty feeling after having to sleep in the car.

Sleeping in the berry field hadn't been all bad, though. When nighttime came, we would crawl into the back of the station wagon, where I would lie on my back next to my dad and look at the ceiling, while he smoked cigarettes (tailor-mades when we could afford it) and talked about what we might do later in the summer, what life had been like before he went broke, why my mother left, why he needed to be with a woman once in a while. But the rest of it— the hard, narrow mattress, the ticking of the wind-up alarm, the cold damp mornings—fell short of being a camping trip like other boys went on.

Going to buy my breakfast at a cafe, then, was a measure of my new status—especially since it was a cafe where I had been to have the thermos filled.

I walked along the sidewalk with my dad's suggestion in mind that I could read about the game in the newspaper. But I knew that the San Francisco papers, which was all we could find in Watsonville, usually covered the L.A. evening games a day late—Saturday night games on Monday, Sunday night games on Tuesday, and so forth. Even so, there was a chance that they might have at least the score, and they might have some news on Koufax. So I bought a newspaper at the drugstore counter, hoping for a headline announcing a Koufax no-hitter or an update on Maury Wills closing in on Ty Cobb.

It was a common conversational topic among people my dad's age to recall where they were when they heard the news about Pearl Harbor. My dad was walking into a restaurant. One of his friends claimed to have been drinking in a bar called the Alamo, which was believable only because I could easily imagine that guy in a bar on a Sunday morning. Later in my own life, I would remember that I was picking oranges in Visalia, having skipped school for the day, when we heard that President Kennedy had been shot. I was in the sultry Merced County jail when I heard that Elvis was gone. But on this day in August, 1962, I was standing outside a drugstore when I read that Marilyn Monroe had died.

That news in itself was stunning, and it put Koufax and the Dodgers out of my mind. Marilyn Monroe had just come alive for me two days earlier, on a Saturday in the barbershop, when I read a *Life* magazine story about her. And now she was dead, the paper said, from an overdose of pills. I had heard a lot of talk about her and had seen photographs, but as yet I hadn't seen any of her movies—actually, I hadn't realized that she was specifically an actress until I read the article in *Life*.

As I ate my breakfast, which by now had dwindled in importance for me, I browsed through the paper. I was not yet much of a newspaper reader, except for the sports section, but I read all of the stories about her. One of them quoted the *Life* article, where she said, "Fame will go by and, so long, I've had you fame." I remembered having read that line. I thought it was sad for a person to end that way. The paper said she was young, and although I didn't have a clear idea of what kind of an age thirty-six was, I knew she was younger than both my folks, and that seemed pretty crummy.

I didn't feel like going back to the cabin after breakfast, partly because I felt even more morose than before, and partly because I wanted to give my dad plenty of time to get rid of the pretty Mexican lady. I went to the park where on weekends I played baseball, and as I expected, the park was empty. I set the newspaper beside me on a bench, and as the sun came out, I sat there thinking about whatever came to mind—the field where I would be back picking green beans at this time tomorrow, the labor contractor's truck that would take us there in the morning dark, the lunch pail my father would use for smuggling fresh beans from the field, the possibility of getting an electric radio, Marilyn, the ground ball that had hit me in the mouth two weeks earlier, the Mexican lady, peeing on the geraniums, and back to the beanfield.

I became aware that there was a girl about my age sitting on the edge of the merry-go-round. She was keeping an eye on two little children playing in the sand, and she was sitting sort of sideways with her left leg hiked up over her right leg. She was wearing shorts, turquoise-colored shorts, and a sleeveless white blouse. She had her hair ratted in what some people called a bouffant, and she was putting on lipstick with the aid of a little mirror. She screwed the cap on the lipstick, put it in her purse, drew out a pack of cigarettes, and looked around. She smiled at me and lit a cigarette, then returned to watching the kids.

She seemed to be almost studying them. As I in turn stared at her, she scratched the outside of her left thigh; in doing so, she moved the hem of her shorts to display the white border of what I knew to be a pair of panties.

Something changed in me that instant, even as she smoothed out her turquoise shorts. It wasn't like dropping your pencil in the classroom for a sneak look. There was something I could almost feel, like an energy current, across the space between us. I would have given anything, anything, to have the nerve to get up and go over and sit by her. I wanted to put my hand on that left thigh, do more than just look into that sleeveless blouse.

I wanted to tell her I was almost sixteen, which meant I would soon be able to drive by myself. It also meant I could work on a ladder or drop out of school, or both. I didn't want to tell her the last two, or that we followed the crops and slept in the car. I wanted to tell her my name was Jim. I wanted to smoke one of her cigarettes and talk to her about Marilyn Monroe.

Instead, I sat there and watched her and waited for it all to subside—the tingle, the ripple, the awe. After a little while, she took a kid in each hand and led them past, so that I got a nice profile. She said "Hi" and walked away.

* * * * *

That evening at supper, I asked my dad if we could get an electric radio, a plug-in type. He said we might be able to find a second-hand one pretty easily, for a couple of dollars, as long as he didn't have to listen to the ball game every damn night. I said I didn't mind listening to it outside or in the car, but on nights when he was out, I could hear it inside. He repeated that we could probably find one cheap.

Later, after we had gone to bed but before we turned out the lights, as my father smoked a cigarette, he exhaled slowly and said, "I'm sorry I made you sleep outside last night."

"That's O.K.," I said. "I understand."

"It's nice of you to say that, Jim."

"I didn't mind."

"You didn't seem very happy all day."

"It's O.K."

"You realize . . . that I might ask you to do it again some time?"

"Yeah. I understand."

"Well, maybe you do, but you'll understand better as time goes on."

"I'm beginning to understand."

He patted me on the leg, from outside the blankets. "We do all right together, Jim." Then he put out his cigarette, rolled over and shut off the light, and said good night. I said good night to him.

It was a curious feeling, as I lay there in the bed next to my father, to sense that he was no longer my Daddy. He was my father. My Daddy was the one who used to hold my hand when we crossed an intersection. My father was the one I worked beside in the fields. If he bought whiskey, I got soda pop and candy. When he bought a men's magazine, I got a battery for the transistor radio, and now I would have a radio of my own.

On the radio I would learn that Koufax was sidelined for the rest of the year, and at the end of the season I would listen to the Giants edge out the Dodgers for the pennant. But Koufax came back the next year to no-hit the Giants, and then to demolish the Yankee dynasty almost single-handedly in the World Series.

Later in life I would lose my father for good, and I would gain and lose a wife through marriage and divorce. Life has seemed to me a long series of gains and losses, some less gradual than others; but I don't believe I ever gained and lost so much in so short a time as I did on that one day in August shortly before I turned sixteen.

Like a Cat Full of Ham

One of the tolerable features of the bunkhouse, in addition to its being warm and dry and well lighted, was that a fellow didn't have things forced on him. Tony had been in the bunkhouse long enough to know the patterns and the rules. In the evenings and on days like today, when it was too wet to pick oranges, the middle-aged men would gather around the table at the end of the room, where they would bring out their hoards of small change. A fellow was welcome to sit in on the two-bit-limit game, or, like the kid Johnny, he could sit on the fringe and watch. Earl, in grey sideburns and western shirt, insisted that it was no bother—the kid could watch him as he played his hand. This Johnny did, and he seemed to be learning the game. He was also learning to roll cigarettes.

Or, if a fellow wanted, he could relax on his own cot and read whatever stray magazine or paperback lay around. That was when the low-level aggravation set in. The chatter in the game was so predictable that Tony could read *Heller With a Gun* and follow the game at the same time. The man on Earl's left, each time the deal came to him, would declare in a half-question, "How 'bout a little high-low?" If no one declared, "Cut 'em thin so someone can win," then it was "Cut 'em deep and somebody'll weep." In a game of five stud, as each card was slapped down, the same voice called them off: every deuce was a duck, every five was a feever, every queen was a whore, and every king was a cowboy. Spades were shovels; clubs, puppy tracks. If three eights were out, there was heavy speculation on who had the case eight. Behind all of this, a cheap radio whined a country-western station.

Alternately with the poker game lingo, and largely for Johnny's benefit, Tony suspected, was the pitter-patter about women. He became aware that he had read several pages of *Heller With a Gun* and had not followed the story, following instead Vernon's yarn about a "nigro" girl—how he had given her a ride in his father's wagon, how this was in Texas and drawn by horses yunnerstan', how he had glimpsed her panties when she climbed up into the buckboard, how his father had walked in on them in the barn, how the nigro girl had scuttled out from under him just like that, how his father like to beat him till the blood run. The moral: "But if you ever get a chance to sample some of that, Johnny, give it a try." "They say it changes yer luck." "They say a lot of things." And so on, around the table.

Tony picked up his matches and Marlboros from the little bedstand, lit a cigarette, tore off the front of the matchbook cover, and stuck it for a marker at the beginning of chapter seven. He swung his feet to the floor, his back to the poker game. Three bunks away, Percy seemed to be having better luck reading *Travels With Charley*. Seemed to be, anyway.

Percy did as well at minding his own business as anyone Tony had ever met. He didn't talk about himself much, but from a scrap that he dropped here and there and from a few comments by the other men, Tony had gathered that Percy had once had a wife who had left him, a son who had left him, and a teaching career of some sort that had slipped through his hands. As a rule, he did not drink in the bunkhouse, but between jobs he laid up in a town like Sacramento or Marysville for a minor amount of whoring and a major amount of drinking.

The other men would have gathered this from one season to the next here in the bunkhouse, or at other camps along the way. This was Percy's fourth or fifth year in the corner, Earl's tenth at the poker table. Later in the year they would cross paths, perhaps in the apricots in late spring, peaches in mid-summer, or pears and apples into the fall. Tony could easily picture these same men and others, maybe in the apple harvest up in Ya-kima—Earl dealing the cards and ribbing the man on his right for giving the deck a whorehouse cut; Vernon telling Johnny how it was with a woman; Percy not at the table but reading a book, perhaps coming out of seclusion to play a two-handed game of gin or casino.

Tony pictured himself too easily in that group, following the fruit, too old to take life like Johnny, too young to talk to the fruit tramps about Roosevelt and the War, hemorrhoids, impotence, or what it had been like when everybody picked in field crates, not these damn bins, and there weren't so many Mexicans. He didn't relish the picture, yet he knew that each of these men had probably given a try, from time to time, at getting together enough money to change. Maybe they, too, had slipped past twenty-five and had definite notions of where they wanted to be at thirty, then had glided past that. Tony imagined there were others like Percy, with stories more effectively buried, who had made it by thirty, lost it by forty, and were hanging on at fifty and looking back in silence.

Tony found himself gazing absently at Percy, when the older man looked up, as if he were looking over reading glasses or once had.

"Find a good stopping place, Tony?"

"Yeah. How's your book?"

"Pretty good. Pretty good. Poor guy just died, you know—Steinbeck. Just before Christmas."

"Is that right."

"Yep. Not very old. Good writer, though." Percy had the book closed on his stomach, with his finger holding the place. "Yep," he said, sitting up, "good writer."

Each bedstand was different. Percy's was a field crate standing on end, with two shelves tacked inside. He set the book on the upper of the two shelves, then took his pipe from the oval-shaped mackerel can on top.

Tony watched him stuff the pipe and light it. "What do you think of a cup of coffee, Percy?"

"Sounds just fine."

"I'll bring it. Black, right?"

"That's right." Percy smiled and settled back on his cot, hands crossed on his stomach.

When Tony came back with the coffee, he took Earl's cot, across from Percy's. "Well, Percy, do you have any plans on where to go after the oranges are done?"

"Oh, I can't say as I plan that much."

"What did you do last year?"

"I found a pretty good job working for a lady down by Lodi. Widow lady. She had a vineyard. Wine grapes. I worked pruning grape vines, fixing the wires they grew on, hoeing weeds, doing little things. Good job."

"Why don't you go back there?"

Percy smiled and tinkered with his pipe. "Oh," he said, "that lady was too nice."

"Too nice?"

"Yeah. In a couple of ways. All polite, I mean. But she would bring out coffee and rolls on the back patio, and I would sit there and take a long coffee break and just talk about anything with her."

"That sounds nice enough."

"Oh, it was. She liked my work—said she did. Said she liked having a fellow around who was more than a field hand. I did other little odd jobs, like trimming a door or fixing faucets. She liked that. And she liked to talk, to have a civilized conversation."

"Did she run out of work for you?"

"No, not at all. But she asked me one day—" Percy lowered his voice, looked at the poker table, stoked his pipe, and drew his brows together. "She asked me if I thought I'd ever marry again."

"Oh."

"She was too nice, you see, and I had nothing to bring to it. Not a thing."

"Jesus, that would be hard to pass up."

"I lived like that once. Nice home and all that, very respected. But when you've had it once, you don't want to go through it and ruin it all over again. At least I don't."

Tony didn't answer. He turned it over in his mind. It was unlike Percy to reveal that much. It was also his first indication that the loss of his marriage was anything but his wife's fault.

"Yeah," Percy said, breaking the silence, "it's more of a comfort to think about what might have been." He flicked his eyebrows. "And you, what do you think you'll do when we pull out of here?"

"Depends on how much of a stake I have. With this weather it's pretty slow."

"It sure is. What do you think the chances are that we pick this afternoon?" Percy had brought them back around to easy conversation.

"I don't know. It's stayed pretty wet with all this fog, and the sun hasn't come out yet."

"We'll likely find out after lunch."

"Probably so. I wouldn't mind making at least board and room today."

"It *would* be nice." Percy re-lit his pipe. "Sometimes it makes you feel for the family man."

"Sure does." Tony looked into his coffee cup, empty now. "More coffee, Percy?"

"No, thanks. I've had enough. But get yourself another cup."

As he tinkered with the coffee urn, the sugar, and the powdered cream, Tony did think of the family man. He wouldn't have thought to, but Percy's comment brought it back to him, how it had seemed to him that morning as they all waited to find out it was too wet. For it had been family men who had stood up and bunched together, leaving their picking bags on the benches in front of the company store. Under the yard light in the dark winter morning, they waited for the boss's word.

"Too wet. Way too damn wet," he said, stepping out of the company pickup. "You men on the pruning crew, get your gear. You men in the bunkhouse, check back at ten." He looked at a man who came to work with his two boys, boys who hoped to work for grocery money but who no doubt hoped for a reprieve from mud and cold fingers and a heavy daylong sack around the neck. "You folks as drove in, you can wait around, I guess."

The father took nerve, and said, "Could you put me on pruning?" The superintendent looked inconvenienced, as if those who didn't live in company housing were a bother. The boys' father added, "Just me. The boys'll wait in the car."

"O.K.," the big boss granted. "Go ahead. Check out some pruning shears and a saw."

The father stood in front of the Dutch door between the store and the superintendent's office, the boys went to sit in the old Buick, the big boss went into his office, and the bunkhouse men, having waited out the last lingering words of the boss, went back down the steps to their basement quarters. Meanwhile the other family men, the ones who lived in the metal-sided, metal-roofed, plastic-windowed company housing, were returning with their shears and saws. Tony had stayed to finish his cigarette and to ponder the old Filipino man who had sat on the bench all this time smoking a cigar, who had not gotten up to hang on the boss's every word, who had brought his shears and his folding saw in his picking bag, and who had the largest family of all.

At ten o'clock, Johnny and Tony went back up to hear the word. The pruning crew was still out, and the two boys were snoozing in the Buick. Tony opened the superintendent's door and peeked in. The boss looked up from one of two opened ledgers. "Check back after lunch."

On the way down the stairs Johnny said, "I don't give a damn if we do work. I don't want to go out if I can't make my hunnerd an' twenty-five bags a day."

They brought the word back to the bunkhouse, and that had been the beginning of the poker game, the tinny radio, and the out-behind-the-barn stories.

Now it was 11:30, forty-five minutes until lunch, an hour and a quarter till the next proclamation. Tony took his cup back to Earl's cot, across from Percy's again.

"Yeah," he said, "at this rate it's gonna take a while to get a stake together."

"Not a bad place to winter, though," Percy answered.

"No, not bad. But I'd like to get a little money ahead, not have it eaten up by board and room, and candy and cigarettes at the company store."

"Well, what does it take just to get by? Forty bags a day?"

"About that. If I could average a hundred bags a day—that's counting some short days and some good days—I could get a car when orange season is over." Tony thought, briefly and bitterly, about how long it would take him, at sixteen cents a bag, to put together a bankroll. Then he wondered how he might guard against peedoodling it away as he had done the last time. To save, and to work each day, he couldn't drink. By not drinking, he was setting himself up for a binge. The fear of ruining it ran as deep as the desire for a drink, or for a clean woman, but the fear was not yet as strong as it seemed to be in Percy.

He looked at Percy, who seemed to be daydreaming. Tony felt he should say something. It was his turn to give it a nudge. "What do you think we'll have for lunch, Percy?"

"Huh?" Percy came out of his daze.

"What do you think we'll have for lunch?"

"Hell, I don't know. Ham."

"Ham?"

"No, not really. But I was just thinking about ham."

"How come?"

"I don't know. You know how it is, I was sitting here thinking about one thing and another, and you know how one idea leads to the next."

"Yeah."

"I was thinking of that lady in Lodi. She had a cat. A nice, big, well-fed cat."

"Uh-huh."

"Reminded me of my wife's cat. When we first got married. I was finishing—" he lowered his voice, glanced again at the card table, "my master's degree. I was doing a research project, another fellow and I, on feral cats. That's cats that have gone back to the wild."

"Oh."

"So we'd go out at night with a spotlight and a .22, out in the countryside. You'd see a lot of interesting things that way."

"I bet."

"We'd shoot a cat or two, whatever we could, and go back to his basement and open them up, to see what they'd been eating. We'd find all sorts of things—mouse fur and bones, bird feathers, grasshoppers—it was fascinating."

"I can imagine."

"Then one night we got a pretty sleek one, and when we opened him up, he was full of ham—fine-grained, boiled ham, it looked like."

"Oh, my God." Tony started laughing, choked on the cigarette he was lighting. "Jesus, what did you do?"

"Oh, my wife raised *hell*. That was the end of that project."

"It wasn't her cat."

"Oh, no. We lived in an apartment in town. This was some old spoiled farmhouse cat, out for a stroll in the moonlight." Percy chuckled. "But she couldn't stand the idea of someone doing that to her little Snookie."

"My God, that's a funny story."

"It sure is. I don't know why I thought of it."

"What did you do to finish the project?"

"Well, since my wife put the kibosh on that project, we came up with another one, trapping ground squirrels. It ended up being easier anyway, but not as interesting."

* * * * *

Lunch turned out not to be ham. It was fried steak, with a large serving of fried potatoes, bell peppers, and onions. Tony spooned fruit-and-jello salad into one corner of the sectioned metal tray, picked out mismatched silverware from the shallow baskets, and sat on the bench next to Percy. He salted his food and soused it with tabasco. Percy poured coffee from a metal pitcher, the kind that jailhouse coffee came served in, but this was better tasting. It occurred to Tony that some of the other men might look at the coffee pitcher that way. The coffee went down the table, crossing paths with a plate stacked with Wonder bread and pats of butter. The men ate as if they had worked all morning and planned to work all afternoon.

After lunch, in the restroom and shower room upstairs from the bunkhouse, where fruit pickers and bosses stood at the same urinal, he met the row boss.

"What does it look like for this afternoon?" Tony asked.

"Big boss says we probably won't pick till tomorrow. But he'll give the word at a quarter till."

He did.

Back downstairs, Tony put on his blanket-lined denim jacket, combed his hair, and was about to tell Percy that he was going to hitchhike into town, when he saw that Percy was asleep. His pipe was in the mackerel can, and he had his hands crossed on his stomach. He looked quite content. Tony remembered how relaxed Percy had looked a few days earlier, when he had sat on the bottom muddy rung of his ladder, resting after eating an orange, while the tractor rattled diesel smell and fumes, and pickers scurried by to empty their bags in the bin trailer. As they called out their numbers, number 129 sat complacent, with his hands folded on his picking bag on his lap.

As Tony walked towards the stairs, he saw Johnny snap open a Zippo and light a neatly rolled cigarette.

"This one's called Hot Chicago," the dealer said. "Some people call it Black Moriah."

Upstairs in the company store, Tony ordered two packs of Marlboros and a Three Musketeers. "Put these on 156." The storekeeper nodded and marked it down.

Walking through the main yard toward the road that led to the highway, and unwrapping the candy bar as he walked, he saw the two boys in the Buick. One of them was reading a school book, which struck Tony as peculiar.

As he walked in the damp air, he reasoned with himself. He had brought only five dollars, and he would not drink; he would shoot pool and maybe have a hamburger. He had enough to buy a couple of beers, too, but he would not drink.

He lit a cigarette, pulling a match from a new book. He thought of the bunkhouse again, and he realized that Percy, asleep on his bunk, had looked like a cat full of ham.

Peach Picking

I steered with one hand and held up the slip of paper with the other, looking at the road and then at the paper to make sure I was going the right way. The lady in the labor office had written "Take River Rd. to Rd 33 turn left go half mile turn right at big barn. Camp in back." Under "Person to Contact," she'd written "Mr. Mullins." It was the Bower Ranch, so I took it that Mr. Mullins was the foreman.

The camp was in back of the old barn all right, amongst some walnut trees, and it looked like it was just about full. There was one long building that looked like a bunkhouse with washrooms at the end, and a house trailer at the other end. Directly in back of the barn, so they would catch the afternoon shade, I guess, were three canvas-covered tents built up on wooden frames. There were cars parked all through the yard—Oldsmobiles, Plymouths, a DeSoto, an old Packard, a couple of Fords, and a '59 Chevy. Seeing all these cars, I figured the foreman must come and pick up the workers and take them to the field.

I went and knocked on the door of what I took to be the bunkhouse, and a big Mexican lady opened the door. That whole smell of a Mexican house—beans, fried tortillas, and all—came drifting out around her, and two little nippers stood beside her and looked up at me. The little boy didn't have pants.

"Hi," I said. "I'm lookin' for the boss, Mr. Mullins."

"No speakin' Inglish."

"*Patrón?*" My Spanish came mostly in single words.

She rattled on a pretty long sentence in a pretty short time, and I picked out that the boss would be back about three. It was one o'clock now and pretty hot, so I got a drink out of the water faucet and sat in the shade of one of the walnut trees. I got bored and went and got a *True Detective* magazine out of my car, but that was pretty stale, so I rolled a cigarette and sat there and looked at nothing. It wouldn't do any good to poke around the camp until I was sure I had a job here.

About three o'clock, a man in a straw hat came driving in on one of those low-slung orchard tractors pulling a flat trailer with people sitting all over it. There were old men, young men, and little kids, most of them Mexicans, some of them sitting with their legs draped over the front and two towhead kids standing up like they were doing the surf. It always gives me the jimmies to see kids with their legs hanging over the side, especially in front, but that was their business and Mr. Mullins', I guess. He stopped the tractor as everybody was hopping off. I went up to him and gave him the slip of paper.

"Labor office sent me out here. Said you could use pickers."

He looked at the slip. "You come from the Marysville office?"

"No, I come from the little trailer they have outside of town here."

"I put in an order at the Marysville office too." I didn't have much of an answer to that, and he didn't seem to expect one. Maybe he expected better people to come from the bigger office. "You picked peaches before?"

"Sure," I said. "Picked peaches, apricots, pears, plums, everything but—"

"O.K. Don't want anyone that don't know what they're doin'."

"You got work, then?"

"I was hopin' to get a family in here. Single man has a hard time keepin' up with the crew."

"I can handle it."

"Maybe I can give you half sets, or put you with this other old boy and his girl." Then he seemed to think better of that. "We'll see in the morning. That your car?" With the slip of paper he pointed at my Dodge.

"Yeah. Where you want me to park it?"

"Over by that other old boy's DeSoto."

"Lady in the labor office said you had a place to stay."

He squinted. "Not a hell of a lot of room here. Don't like to ask you to sleep in your car."

I'd been doing that, and it didn't sound too good. "I'd appreciate a bunk," I said, pushing just a little.

"There's two Mexican families livin' in the house. It's kind of a duplex. White man and Mexican wife in the trailer with their little kids. His kids, the bigger ones, they got one of the tents. Old guy and his girl got the tent on the other end. I hate to give away the only tent to a single man. I was hopin' to get a family in here." He stared at the paper again, as if there was an answer there, and then he looked at me. For the first time I saw his eyes. They were close together, like he could look through a keyhole with both of them at once. They were a washed-out blue. "Tell you what. I'll let you have the tent, but if I get a family in here, we'll have to rig up something else for you."

"That's O.K. with me," I said, glad to get out of my car for at least a day or so. "I can use the washroom over there?"

"Oh yeah," he said. "There's men and women's room both." He seemed to be a little proud of that.

"What time you pick up the crew in the morning?"

"Five-thirty, quarter to six. It's good daylight by six."

I got my stuff laid out in the tent without too much bother. The place had a wooden floor. I put the cardboard box with my clean clothes in one corner, my dirty clothes in a heap in the other corner, and my blankets to one side of the doorway. I used my denim jacket for a pillow usually, and it was clean. I decided I'd rather go a little chilly in the morning than have my pillow all itchy with peach fuzz. That was one thing about peaches, you needed to have a good bath or shower when you got off work. When I had my stuff laid out, I brought in the box with my grub in it, and I dug out some soda crackers and a can of pork and beans. I had a Clorox jug for water, which I went and rinsed out and put fresh water in, and set that on the floor, too. There was already a peach lug in there for a table. I opened the beans and laid out a handful of crackers on the lug box, and had me a supper. Such as it was. I wished I had a Coleman stove, but that was several bins of peaches down the road. And judging from the way I hit it off with Mr. Mullins, it might not be this job that got me the stove.

I was glad for the tent, though, because it kept out most of the mosquitoes. Mosquitoes and peaches always seemed to go together.

I heard the camp rattling around way before sunup. An alarm clock went off in one of the other tents, and I heard the old boy yelling at his daughter to get up and get coffee going. I sure hoped I didn't have to work with them. I imagined them picking the bottoms and outsides, and me picking the middles. If I wanted to do that, I could go back and work with my old man.

It turned out that Mullins gave me a half set and them a half set. "You pick these four trees," he said, "and they can have these four. The two of yuhs can move together, and keep up with the families. One of you finishes first, ask the other if he needs a hand." He shook out a Lucky and lit it, and he smiled for the first time that I saw. "You fill this kid in on anything he needs to know, uh Glenn?"

The old boy, who wore one of those tight-fitting khaki caps, said, "Sure, Dal. He looks like a good boy." He looked at me like it was my fault he started the day off lying like that.

I thought maybe Glenn would pick the tops from the ladder, and the girl would pick the bottoms, but no, it was the other way around. She picked most of the tops, and she crawled inside the crotch of the trees and picked all the middles, too. Glenn puttered around and picked the bottoms, and would squat down and roll himself a cigarette now and again and tell his daughter not to pick the green ones. "Dal don't want none of that goddamn *grass* green, now honey." Every once in a while I'd catch her looking at me, or she'd catch me looking at her, but that always happens when you're working in an orchard. She didn't seem embarrassed like some girls do, to have an old man like that and have to pick fruit for a living. She was kind of pretty, too, it looked like, but I couldn't tell with her all covered up with a cap like her dad's, a loose work shirt, baggy pants, and the picking bag slung across her shoulders. I thought I'd like to see her when she was cleaned up with her blonde hair washed and combed out.

Glenn spoke to me for the first time about two o'clock in the afternoon. I had to take a leak, so I went over a couple of rows behind a low branch and let 'er go. I was just zipping up when a green peach came whistling through the leaves in front of me. Then I heard his voice, which I was familiar with by now.

"You dirty little sonofabitch! Hadn't you got no common decency? Piss like that right in front of this girl? I oughta get you run off this god-damn crew. See how you like that, if it teaches you any manners. Why don't you learn to go back down the row a few trees?"

"I thought I was out of sight enough."

"If I saw you, this girl could, for Christ-sake."

"Sorry," I said. I didn't say anything to her. I was sure she didn't want to hear any more of it than I did.

We didn't have any further conversation for the next two days. I kept my mouth shut, and whenever I finished my half a set—and I always finished ahead of them both—I sat in the shade and took a smoke break or ate my lunch. I was making my four bins a day, which came to fourteen dollars, and that was fine with me. In the afternoon of the third day, he spoke to me again. "Hey, you! Young feller!"

"Yeah?" I was up in the middle of a tree, one leg on my ladder and one leg in the forks of a branch.

"How about you take the rest of our set? We're knockin' off early. I'll tell Dal."

"O.K.," I said, and when I got out of my tree I saw, naturally, that the bottoms had all been picked. He left me half a top and two middles. One thing my dad had taught me, and that was not to pick after no other sonofabitch. I didn't like being pushed around, but I thought maybe this was one way of keeping peace, so I picked it. I still got my four bins that day.

The next day they didn't come to work, so I got full sets, and sure enough I lagged behind the rest of the crew. When Mullins punched my card for the last two bins, he said, "You'll be able to keep up with the crew tomorrow."

"Someone else be with me?" I wondered if he was going to move another single man into my tent, or something like that.

"Nah, Glenn and his girl will be back. He wasn't feeling too well today, and he didn't want to send the girl out alone." He looked at me, and I could tell that Glenn had told him about me taking a leak.

That afternoon, the girl was all scrubbed up clean and sitting in front of their tent in the shade, working on her fingernails. Her old man usually didn't let her out and wander around the camp, it seemed to me, so I thought maybe he was taking a nap. Or sleeping off a drunk, now that I thought of it. I waved to her as I walked to my tent and again as I walked to the shower room. She looked pretty damn cute, all washed up and in a clean shirt and jeans and wearing lipstick. Her blonde hair was shiny and wavy down to her shoulders. She looked about sixteen or seventeen, but that's always hard to tell.

Her dad still wasn't up and about when I came out of the shower, and she was taking some laundry off the clothesline. I knew he couldn't see us from their tent, even if he was awake, so I called over to her. "Day off today, uh?"

"Yeah, Daddy wasn't feeling good at all."

I walked over to her, with my dirty clothes balled up in my hand. "We never did get introduced," I said. "My name's George."

"My name's Viola," she said. That was the first time I'd even heard her name. "Where you from?"

"Oh, I been all around," I said. "Mostly from Bakersfield, I guess. Where you folks from?"

"Back east." She pronounced it "Bike east," which told me either Oklahoma or Arkansas. Not that it mattered.

"Well, enjoy your day off," I said. "See you in the morning." I didn't want to push it any more than that.

"Bye, bye," she said, and it sounded like "Bah, bah."

Sun was just going down and the mosquitoes were starting to come out, and I was sitting in front of my tent smoking a cigarette and thinking about going inside when she came over. There'd still been no sign of her dad. She walked right past me and sort of whispered as she went by, "Meet me around the other side of the barn, where we can talk."

I didn't know what to do. I hated to turn down a chance to get close to her, but I also hated the thought of having another run-in with her old man. He was really a sour old fart. Then I figured the worst thing that could happen would be to have to pack my bags, and that didn't seem like all that bad a deal, so I finished my cigarette and followed her around. "What's on your mind?" I said, as I walked up.

"I came to you because I didn't know who else to go to," she breathed, putting her hand on my arm.

"What about?"

"Can I trust you?"

"Sure," I said. "Well, probably. Dependin'."

"You have to help me."

"Help you what?"

"I want to get out of here."

"You what?"

"I want to get out of here. I hate it here."

"You want to leave your dad?"

She put her hand on my arm and looked at me wide-eyed. "You promise you won't tell anyone, not Dal Mullins or anyone?"

"Tell what?"

"He's not my daddy. He's just keepin' me because he wants to use me. I gotta get out of here. You can help me." She pushed her soft little boob against my arm and it felt young and plush and I felt sorry for her. I was also going to pieces just a little bit. She shifted her weight but still pressed against me. "Please."

* * * * *

Next morning I was working by myself again. I heard them arguing in the middle of the night—he wanted to go to town and wanted her to go with him. "You're not stayin' in this god-damn place by yourself," I heard him say. Then I heard them leave, and come back in about an hour. I didn't hear their alarm go off in the morning, and neither of them showed up to get on the trailer.

Out in the orchard I told Mullins I'd like a draw. He gave me a narrow look through those close-set eyes of his. "You fixin' to pull out?"

"No," I said, "I just need some grub money and a couple of other things."

"Give a man a draw," he said, "and he goes on a drunk."

"Nah, I don't want to go on no drunk. This is my fifth day and I was broke when I got here, and I'm about out of groceries."

"Well," he said, looking me over, "I can get you a draw through yesterday. Boss always likes to hold a day's wages, and I agree with him on that."

"I'd appreciate it."

For the rest of the day, about all I could think of was that girl and the fix she was in. It worked on me. That old man put me in mind of a dog my brother had when we were growing up. My old man had a young bitch pup, and one day when she was about four months old she squatted for a little pee. That old dog came over and sniffed the spot, and raised his leg and covered her spot with his own. Like he was claiming her. It seemed like that old man, whoever he was, was doing the same kind of thing with this girl. It seemed like it was up to me to lift her out of this mess.

I imagined we could go on up to Yakima for the late cherries and then some apricots, then maybe back down to Eugene or Medford for the pears. Just stay out of California for a while. The idea struck me as kind of cozy, the two of us traveling together and sharing a cabin together and working together. One thing about her, I knew she would hold her own in the field and not be a burden. And even if she didn't stay with me but went on to her own folks, at least I could give her the help she needed right now. I'd think about that old man and I'd get burned, and then I'd remember how she'd pushed up against me the night before. She might take to me well enough at that.

In the afternoon when Dal punched my ticket, he handed me a check. I glanced at it and saw that it was for fifty-two dollars and some change.

By the time I got out of the shower, I was starting to get a little tingly about the whole business. First thing I had to do was go to town and get the check cashed. I ate dinner at a little restaurant, did my laundry, and gassed up the car. Back at the labor camp, I parked the car in front of my tent and casually slipped the rest of my clothes and bedding into the back seat. I had a six-pack of Burgie and a pack of tailor-made cigarettes, so I sat there in the dark in that empty tent and punched open a beer and lit a cigarette.

Along about the end of my second beer, she poked her blonde head in through the flap of the tent. "He's asleep," she whispered. "Let's go." I picked up the other four beers and we got into my Dodge and rolled out of there. It was that simple.

I drove for about an hour and was starting to get a little drowsy from the beer when she said, "I can drive for a while if you want."

"You know how to drive?"

"Sure."

I was starting to get wide awake again. "Why don't you scoot over here and help me drive for a while, and then maybe I'll let you drive by yourself."

So she scooted over and put her left foot on the gas and put her hands on the wheel and I kept my left hand on the wheel and put my right arm around her. We wobbled along the highway like that for about twenty miles, and then it wasn't much fun any more.

"Let me drive now," she said.

"You might need a little help, though," I said with a smile.

"No, I can drive by myself."

"But I'll sit close just in case you need some help." So I pulled it over and we changed places, and we were off again. We were almost to Redding when I finished the last beer. I didn't think we'd make it all the way to Oregon that night, so I suggested we pull over.

"What for?"

"I got to use the bushes." Which I did.

"O.K.," she said, and she whipped the Dodge onto the shoulder and damn near spilled us.

"Careful," I said, and got out, leaving her at the wheel and the engine running. Off in the bushes I was a little worried she might take off, except she knew I had the money.

When I got back to the car, she was lighting one of my cigarettes. "Boy, am I glad to get away from him," she said, shooting out a cloud of smoke and dropping the car into gear.

Back on the road she was clipping along at seventy, and every time she went to ash her cigarette, she'd swerve. That made me nervous, and I was glad she hadn't drunk any of the beer.

"Hey," I said, nudging her, "I don't think we'll make it to Oregon tonight. Why don't we get some sleep and get a fresh start in the morning? I think we can make it all the way through Oregon tomorrow, and on to Yakima."

"I want to drive a little farther. Light me another cigarette, will ya?" She ground out the one she'd been puffing on, and the car swerved again.

By and by she got tired, so we pulled over at one of those wide spots where there are picnic tables and garbage cans. "This is as good a place as any," I said. "You want to sleep out under the stars, or in the car?"

"What do you mean?"

By now I was sitting by the passenger door, so I leaned over to put my arm around her and maybe kiss her. "I thought we could have a cozy little bed out on the ground."

She drew back towards her own door. "You mean sleep to-gether?"

"Well, not if you don't want to."

"You just wanted to sleep with me. You wanted to use me."

"No, I didn't—"

"I thought you were nice, that's why I asked you to help me. And now you just want to use me."

"No, that's not it at all, I just thought that if you wanted to—"

"No, I don't want to. If all you want is to use me, then I'll find my own way. I thought you wanted to help me."

I thought she was going to get hysterical. "No, you don't have to go anywhere. I do want to help you. I wanted to help you get away from that old man, that was the main thing." I took

35

the keys and got in the back seat, and handed her a blanket over to the front seat. "Let's just get some sleep," I said. Then after a little silence I said, "I'm sorry if I hurt your feelings. The main thing was, I really did want to get you away from that scum of an old man. It wasn't right him keepin' you like that."

I expected her to at least thank me on that point, but she said, "Now don't you get started saying nasty things about him. Even if he is a dirty old drunk, he's still my Daddy."

* * * * *

I didn't sleep very well at all. Finally about two or three in the morning I drifted into a pretty sound sleep, considering the circumstances. I was having a long and peculiar dream about taking a bath in the river with her and her Daddy and Dal Mullins, all of us naked, when I got woke up by the scrunch of tires sliding in gravel. I sat right up, and all at once I saw it was broad daylight, she was sitting on a picnic bench smoking another of my cigarettes and working on her fingernails, and her Daddy's DeSoto was settling to a stop in a cloud of dust right next to my Dodge.

The first thing he did was he walked over and slapped the cigarette out of her mouth. My front passenger door was open, so I could hear him just fine. "Get your little ass over into that car where you belong!" She just stood there. "Get over there!" Then she started to cry, like she knew he was going to hit her. "And don't start your god-damn bawlin', neither."

I got out of the car and stood there in my stocking feet. I was glad I had my pants on. "I'm sorry about this, Glenn," I started.

"Don't you even talk to me, you dirty little bastard." I could see he hadn't gotten off his drunk yet.

"I guess it's my fault," I said. "She asked me to, and I—"

"Yeah, and you were just enough of a god-damn fool to do it." He turned to her as she started to walk towards his car. "And you," he said, "next thing you know you'll be gettin' knocked up. Stupid little bitch." He looked at me again. "The both of you's as dumb as a day-old nigger. You want her to get knocked up?"

She got into his car and slammed the door, then rolled down the window and hollered out, "No, Daddy! He didn't! He was just giving me a ride. He didn't . . . *use* me!" She rolled up the window.

"All I can say to you, you little sonofabitch, is you're god-damn lucky you didn't." Then, as if he was pleased with himself for putting it so well, he repeated, "You're just god-damn lucky you didn't!" He crawled into his DeSoto, cranked it up, and spun out of there. He made a big arc and rattled gravel all over my car and the picnic table, and as his tires dug onto the highway, he squealed away to the south. I could see him leaning over towards her, his head jerking up and down as he gave her his mind.

I sat back down in the back seat of my car and put my shoes on, then lit a cigarette and sat there smoking it. It seemed hard to argue with him on that last point, what with the kind of trouble that girl could make. But after I'd thought it all over a little more, he didn't seem all that much in the right, either. As I ground out the snipe on the floorboard, I thought a little poozle probably wouldn't have done any harm at all.

Gunfight at Mesquite Creek

The landlord had been courteous, in his own blunt way, and had agreed to let the little house go for a year. With the first and last months' rent, he didn't even care for a deposit. He explained how the pump worked, where the septic tank was, and where the fuse box was. In addition, he showed Pete the garden shed and gave him a rundown on what dusts to use for the shrubs and vegetables—if he cared to put in a garden. He had plenty of cats at his place, he said, and Pete could have one for the mice, if he wanted. There was a great walnut tree in back and, yes, that would be nice shade for rabbits. Pete had suggested that he might like some rabbits.

When the landlord drove away in his pickup, Pete found an old field crate and took it into the living room. Sitting there on the crate, he looked around him and placed his furniture here and there. The desk would do well over there by the window, the plants under the south window, the armchair maybe where he was sitting now, and the record player, some book shelves, and so forth . . . yes, this would do very nicely. As he sat there building his new little world, he remembered another world he wanted to work on. He went out to his car and brought back a notebook.

Jade Slade rode into Wichita on a horse. He slouched in the saddle, with his shoulders drooped forward and his hat brim pulled down over his eyes. Occasionally he spat tobacco juice off to his left, and every once in a while he gave a pat to his left hip pocket.

Pete could think of no better possible beginning for a story. He smiled. It was the old intruder plot all over again, to be sure, but there were lots more good stories to be turned on that situation. He felt no call to be squeamish about a little indulgence in convention. When the furniture got here, he would make out a separate folder for this one—*Showdown at Arroyo Gulch*—and it would go in the bottom right drawer. And with time, the folder would grow and fatten. There was a lot of fine work to be done at this place.

He drove into town in his car, hitting quite a few butterflies on the way. A couple of them smeared on the windshield, leaving streaks of what might have been alfalfa. The service station man would clean them off. Once in town, Pete drove around to get a new feel of the place. He found the station he'd stopped at before, when he had come for the interview. The same man leaned into his window with the same name tag, the same leathered face, and the same decayed teeth; as before, he asked the same question.

"Fillerup for ya today?"

"Yeah. Regular." Maybe he should work on saying "yep." He got out of the car and stretched. It was a hot, shimmering day, with the trees green and shady and still, but waving in the heat. *Hotter'n a two-dollar pistol*, he thought. He looked at Larry, realized that he sort of liked him, and took a step toward friendship. "You sure got a lot of bugs here."

"Yep. Now's the time they're thick as thieves." He was doing a good job on the headlights and had already made the windshield shiny and beautiful, so Pete was willing to overlook a misused metaphor.

"Goin' north or south?" Larry asked.

"Neither, actually. I'm thinkin' on stayin' a while."

"Work in the hay?" Larry didn't seem to expect a positive answer.

"No, I'm supposed to start teaching at the high school in the fall."

"Ah, schoolteacher. You're not the new football coach?"

"No, I'm afraid not. I teach English."

"Ah, English. I never did worth a damn at that. That's pronouns and all that shit, ain't it?"

A laugh on Pete's part. "Well, yeah, in a way. You do have to give the kids grammar."

"Let me top off the tank here. You know, if you're plannin' on stayin' around here, you ought to get a screen for your radiator. Keep them damn bugs out."

"That might be a good idea. You carry them here?"

Of course he did. After he had cut off the bottom and tied the screen on, he filled out the credit card slip and Pete signed it.

"Thanks a lot, Mr. Duncan."

"Call me Pete. I'll be comin' in again. Let the kids do all the Mister stuff." He started the car and was just about to put it in gear when Larry spoke again.

"Stayin' in town?"

"Nope. Rented a house out on Leighton Road."

"Gus Dominguez's place. Lot of mosquitoes out there in another month."

* * * * *

The furniture came the next day, and Pete, working up a sweat, resolved to buy a swamp cooler. It could go in the kitchen window. After his shower he still sweated, but he didn't mind it. He thought it came with the territory.

* * * * *

Jack Neill was a healthy-looking fat man, with strong arms and a red face. He smoked his cigarette with gusto as he explained how to hook up the cooler. The old kind just dripped from the top, but this one had a little plastic pump. So you had two switches, one to turn the squirrel cage and one for the pump. You could hear the pump going, but you shouldn't run it without water. Pete bought a hammer and a pound of nails, to build a stand. Jack got onto the teacher subject, too.

"Yeah, last English teacher they had, she wanted to teach poetry and all that shit. Kids came out of there and still couldn't spell. You write?"

"Ah, well, yeah, a little. Mostly essays and columns, you know. About morality, and social values, and that sort of thing." *No end to this teacher business*, he thought.

* * * * *

The following week, on Wednesday, Pete went into town for the weekly livestock auction. He thought it would offer another glimpse of local life, and he thought he might buy an animal to keep in the back yard. Not a cayuse, of course. As the stands around the auction ring began to fill up, Pete observed the crowd. He picked out the small local farmers, with boots down at the heels and hats crumpled at the brim. They sat with their wives and towhead kids. Pete also identified the larger ranchers, often father and son, who were dressed a little better. Their boots were crusty, too, but their hats were in better shape. It seemed odd to Pete that several of the ranchers wore caps. And then there were the commercial stockmen—professional buyers and sellers who wore unsoiled boots, pressed Western shirts, and creased jeans. Some wore dark glasses, quite a few had small pocket notebooks of tooled leather, and most had pocket calculators. So these were the new cattle barons. For the most part they bought in large lots, and they gave their bids with a furtive wave of the finger or a nod of the brim. The small farmers he noticed, bid on one or two animals at a time. *Sodbusters*, he thought.

The baby calves ran through first, followed by the pigs. There were hundreds and hundreds of swine, with long snouts and short ones, straight ears and floppy ears, fat jowls, and tight hams. Pete was amused that the hog buyers bore a striking resemblance to their commodity: jowls and squinty eyes, and shirts as tight as pigskin across their bellies.

When the pigs had gone through, the crowd changed for the sheep. A few goats came through in the meanwhile—nannies with prodigious bags and teats, billies with long horns and flowing beards, and bouncing kids. The idea of owning one of those curious fellows appealed to Pete's imagination, but he held off. When the sheep came, he kept track of the prices and finally bid on a lamb. He fluttered his hand up when the bid came back, but on the third time he dropped out. Several sheep later, he bid on two more lambs, and this time he held the bid. The two little lambs walked out the other gate, and one of the men in the ring handed Pete a slip of paper.

When the crowd shifted again after the sheep, he stayed for the cattle. A new auctioneer came in, a man who measured up to the big buyers who now reassembled. The bidding picked up, the ring men cracked their whips, and Pete saw a whole pageant of dairy cows, beefy steers, and tremendous bulls. The afternoon was wearing on, and he saw through the gates that there were hundreds of cattle to come. He got up and left, and the auctioneer's rhythm faded away as Pete went out of the arena. In the sales office, he paid for his lambs; in return, he was given the sales slip, along with directions for picking up his animals.

Outside, the afternoon was hot and dry. Masses of cattle milled and bawled in the corrals, while men on horses drove them through the alleys. The crack of whips mixed with the "heeyah" of the cowboys and the deep thump of hooves against corral planks. Dust and the smell of dry manure mixed with the hot afternoon, and under the wide, hazy sky, Pete felt puny in the presence of hundreds of tons of beef. He handed his slip to a wizened old cowboy, who shuffled down one of the corral lanes. In the shade of an empty canopied corral, there lounged a young cowboy, standing by his horse and drinking a bottle of beer. When the old man came back with Pete's two lambs, the young cowboy sauntered over and leaned on the corral to look at Pete.

"You got a truck 'n' trailer to haul all that stock in?" Pete did not hear much friendliness in his tone.

"Nah, I think I can get these home in my car."

"Well, if that's the way you do it, I'd suggest one thing. You oughta think about keepin' 'em out on the porch later on. Them sheep get to smellin' up the house after they get to about six months or so."

"Thanks. I'll keep that in mind." Sometimes, thought Pete, there's not much to say to a smart ass.

On the way home, Pete stopped at the feed store, where he bought a bag of grain and picked up a pamphlet on raising lambs. That evening, Gus Dominguez helped him build a pen for the little ones. Gus had a few bits of advice, such as how much hay to feed them, what kind of salt to buy, and how to keep the dogs out. Pete gathered that dogs strayed a long way.

* * * * *

Chapter 15: Jade Slade rode out of Wichita on his horse, with a price on his head, gold in his saddlebags, his six-gun tied tight to his hip . . . and a half-bottle of whiskey.

Pete didn't like to quit writing at the end of a chapter, so he started the next one before putting away the folder. If *Showdown at Arroyo Gulch* turned out the way he liked, maybe the next story could feature the timeless feud between cattlemen and sheepherders. But Jade Slade—gambler, soldier of fortune, wanderer of the frontier—had other problems to solve. There was Jim Mason, the huge, handsome, cold-blooded cattle baron who had an iron grip on Wichita. There was also Betsy Fleming, who feared Jade because she did not know him and who had yet to know what Mason was really made of. But all that in its place; tonight was a night to go into town.

The Alamo was the main bar in town. Pete observed and appreciated the large old mirror with pillars and a high arch framing it in. Animal heads and horns ranged along the walls, from moose to elk to deer to mountain goats. Pete saw steer horns as well. Although the saloon lacked sawdust on the floor and a rinky-dink piano, it did have double doors. Pete had dropped by in the daytime and had seen the card table, but tonight was the first time he'd been in when there was action. He saw a poker game in progress. To Pete's disappointment, however, the band drowned out any table talk he might have picked up from where he stood. He ordered a shot of bar whiskey—three fingers Red Eye, or so it seemed at the moment—and took it over to watch the card game. The table was full at present, and the game seemed friendly. Two of the players had a few chips left, and two others each had a sizeable stack. Pete recognized one of the winners as the condescending young cowboy from the auction; the other players called him Randy, with noticeable respect. Pete told the dealer he'd like a seat when one opened up, and he went back to the bar.

As he pulled the barstool towards him and slid onto it, he saw something he hadn't seen earlier—a slender, dark-haired woman about his own age. The band was singing "The tears have washed 'I Love You' from the blackboard of my heart," and the lady was tapping her cigarette lighter in time. From under dark eyelashes she glanced at him, and he glanced back. The poker game faded far into the background as Pete turned over a dozen possible lines. Presently he came up with what seemed the right one, and he moved over so that only one stool separated them. Between songs he leaned her way. "If I knew your name, I'd feel better about asking you to dance."

"My name's Nancy. Nancy Silva."

Therefore the dark hair and lashes. In the short time since he had come to this town, Pete had sharpened up on the local types. Here was a Portuguese beauty, probably the daughter of a dairyman and maybe a former princess of the annual Portagee Picnic.

"My name is Pete Duncan."

"Are you new here, or from out of town?"

"I'm new here." With a pang of regret he added, "School-teacher."

"Oh." The tone was as neutral as a child chanting his vowels.

"But I still wouldn't mind dancing."

"You might talk me into it." She lit a cigarette and took a sip on her drink as the band started "The Tennessee Waltz." Pete stood up, raised his eyebrows, and motioned with his head. She put her cigarette down, and within a few seconds he was waltzing with Nancy Silva. After the dance they returned to the bar, where Pete ordered two more drinks. He was tinkering with the idea of offering to move to a table, when he realized there was a third person standing by them. He turned to meet the cowboy face to face, and he found himself shaking hands.

"This is Randy Collins. This is Pete . . ."

"Duncan."

"You're the sheepherder," said Randy, giving Pete's hand an iron squeeze. It was a squeeze that would, to use a dairyman's saying, bring him to his milk. As he withdrew his hand, Pete felt that it had indeed been squeezed dry.

"Actually, I'm a schoolteacher. But I did take your advice about the lambs. Can I buy you a drink?"

"I've got one at the table. I just came over to tell you there's a seat open." Pete was reluctant to leave Nancy behind, but he was anxious to play cards—even with Randy. He picked up his drink and nodded to Nancy. "I guess I'll see you later on. I'm going to play cards for a while." As Pete sat down with his stack of chips, he noticed Randy hadn't returned. He was having a dance with Nancy.

The poker game was good-natured enough, even when Randy came back. To Pete's surprise, the cowboy rode everyone about the same; but from the tone of Randy's pronouncing "Pete," he would just as soon be called sheepherder or school-teacher. He played a conservative game, and he kept from antagonizing Randy or any of the other players. He knew, though, that a head-on with Randy was inevitable, and he was game for it. After he had played for about an hour and picked up a few more chips, it happened. The man on his right was dealing, and Pete opened for two dollars. Everyone folded but the cowboy, who raised two dollars.

"Get a little of that sheepherdin' money," he said, tossing out four green chips.

Pete called and drew one to a joker flush.

Randy grinned and asked, "Got the Okie buster workin' for ya?"

"Might want to buy some more sheep if I catch it." He didn't look at his cards until he watched Randy draw two.

The cowboy covered his cards without looking at them and said, "Your bet."

As Pete looked at his cards, he felt Randy studying him. There was a fifth club, sweet as you please. "Four dollars."

Randy glanced at his own cards, looked up at Pete, and said, "Back four."

This was getting pretty steep, compared to what the game had been. Pete looked at his cards again and then at his stack, where he saw seven green chips left. He hefted them and spread them out on his side of the pot. "Three more. I'm in."

Randy tossed in his chips. "I call. Let's see what you got."

Pete turned over his flush as nonchalantly as possible.

The dealer screwed up his face and looked the hand over. "Puppy tracks, Randy. Need a full house to beat it." Pete was getting the pot added up in his mind when Randy turned over three deuces and two jacks.

"Guess that does it," Pete said, flipping his cards over and into the center, and pushing back from the table.

Randy looked up from raking in the chips. "You leavin'?"

"Yep. Not catchin' good enough cards. Think I'll go back to dancin'."

"Hate to bust you out of the game."

"Ah, if I think Lady Luck is smilin' on me later on, I might be back." Pete didn't mind rubbing him just a little.

"Okee-doke. You take good care of them lambs, now." Randy finished raking in the chips.

"I aim to." Pete nodded at the table in general and added, "Nice gamblin' with you, gentlemen."

Back at the bar he found Nancy, who asked, "Big winner tonight?"

"Nope. Other way around. Thought I'd try my luck at dancin' again."

She turned to blow away smoke and crush her cigarette, and then she looked him straight in the eye. With a faint, coquettish toss of the head she said, "Win some and lose some, they say."

After a few dances, when he was restored by her perfume and by the slight pressure of her breasts against him, he figured he was even in the game. Smoke was hanging thick in the bar, but he was able to see himself in the mirror. He finished his drink and pushed off of his stool. "Think I'll head home now. Nice meetin' you, and maybe I'll give you a call."

"Yeah, do that." She wrinkled a smile at him.

Pete walked out of the Alamo and got into his car. As he drove out of town, he reflected that he would probably remember the Alamo for a little while to come.

* * * * *

Chapter 21: Jade Slade lay sprawled in the arroyo, watching the hot sun glisten on the blood trickling from his right thigh. In a few hours it would be dark, and he could crawl to the spot where his horse lay. Then he could wash out the wound with what remained of his whiskey.

The breeze from the swamp cooler came through the door from the kitchen into the living room, ever so lightly ruffling the papers on the desk. Pete sipped on his Jack Daniel's and relished the work he had done on *Showdown*. The plot was moving along just fine and not hanging him up. He had his hero right where he wanted him for the time being—shot out of the saddle and out of reach of his Winchester—so he closed the folder and put it away.

Nancy had sounded enthusiastic over the phone when she agreed to meet him at the Alamo. As there was no band on Wednesday night, Pete looked forward to a cozy, quiet conversation. He tossed off the rest of his drink, reflected alternately on the virtues of Jack Daniel and Jade Slade, and spruced up for another night in town. He thought about wearing a hat, then thought better of it.

Nancy was sitting at a table when he arrived, and in the dim light she looked—maybe a little sad, but charming. Something burned in him, and he knew it wasn't the Jack Daniel's. She smiled and tapped her cigarette in the ashtray when he sat down. Pete ordered two drinks, and the conversation settled down from how are you to how do you like living in our town.

"It's an interesting place. Quiet, almost sleepy. I like it quite a bit. Sort of legendary."

"What do you mean by that?"

"Oh, I don't know. I just have a hard time thinking of it by its real name."

"How do you think of it?"

"Some—well—legendary type of name. Ringo Junction, Poison Creek, Hangin' Rock—you know. The town is more picturesque than its name, Owensville."

"Oh."

There was that neutral tone again. Pete was glad he'd kept the name Mesquite Creek to himself. Too cute.

Nancy's voice came back. "Why did you come here to teach school? What is it you teach?"

He thought he had told her before, but he said, "English. Pronouns and all that."

"Why did you come here?"

"I liked the looks of the town when I came for the interview, and I guess they liked my looks. Anyway, they offered me the job." *My God*, he thought, *I have to get off this topic. I'll be talking about my sheep next.* "Tell me about our friend Randy Collins. He seems interesting." Pete studied her casually.

"Randy's a pretty nice guy. A little rowdy sometimes, but he just likes to feel his oats."

"Is he a real cowboy?"

"He has cattle, and he rides his horses. What do you mean?"

"I guess that's what I mean. He doesn't get into gunfights or swing from the chandeliers, I'm sure."

"He did do one funny thing in here about a month ago." She started laughing and took a sip. "There were some hay haulers in here—you know, the types that talk with an Okie accent. Well, Randy was feeling pretty good, so he walked over to the one wearing a hat and took the hat off his head. 'Anyone that talks as stupid as you do,' he said, 'ought to have two holes cut in his hat.' So he took out his pocket knife and cut two holes in the guy's hat, and put it back on his head. 'For your god-damn dumb-ass donkey ears to stick out of,' he said. Everyone in here just about died laughin'." Nancy started laughing again.

Pete smiled. *A real Brom Bones type of village bully*, he thought. "What did the hay hauler do?"

"Oh, nobody messes with Randy."

It occurred to Pete that he was well off leaving his hat at home. He'd have to work his way up to that status.

A few drinks and a couple of hours of nondescript conversation slipped by, and it was time to leave. Pete walked her to her car and opened the door for her. With one hand on the corner of her door and the other on her waist, he leaned in to kiss her on the cheek. As he leaned back again, she laid her right hand, open, flat against the front of his shoulder.

"You should come to dinner some time."

"I should. Yes, I should. Weekend or week night?"

"How about next Wednesday?"

"A week from tonight. Sure. What time?"

"Make it around seven or seven-thirty."

"Fine. I'll see you then."

* * * * *

Jade Slade thumbed the hammer on his Colt, and at almost the same instant he saw Jim Mason reel away with the impact. He thought he heard the slug bury into the huge-barreled stomach of the range boss, but he was actually feeling the shock of Mason's bullet thudding into his own side. Now his ears were dull from the roar of gunfire, and the pain, which was at first delayed, came on in all its rawness and strength. He dropped first to his knees, all the while keeping his eyes on Mason . . . but Mason was not moving. No doubt he was lying there, eyes wide open to the stars. He was barely visible, slumped on the other side of the campfire, but he did not move,

53

not even in the last throes of death. Jade's aim had been true, and Mason was dead—that much was certain. He dropped now to his stomach, and he took his rest there. He turned his eyes to the fading campfire and fancied that he saw her dancing in the coals. In a few hours it would be morning, and Betsy would be here; after that everything would be fine. He slept.

The End

This was strange business, jotting down "The End" to *Showdown*. In the past week, Pete had written the last five chapters, and now he wondered if he hadn't rushed it just a little. He wasn't sure, for one thing, if the story was a response to his own little intrigue, or if it was an unwitting anticipation of what was yet to come. No doubt there was a connection, but he didn't know which way it worked. Either way, he wasn't sure he should have finished it. Jade had settled his score, and that was all good and fine, but had the ending come too easily? He still had over an hour this evening before dinner at Nancy's, and as he tucked the folder away, he figured he would stew on the problem and take his time shaving. And there was always time for revision, if it turned out he was jumping the gun.

* * * * *

Nancy served a ranch-style dinner of pork chops, salad, and green beans, rounded out with fresh dairy milk and Portuguese spice cake. Once again Pete brought up the topic of Randy Collins.

Nancy didn't seem to mind. "Randy and I have always been good friends. We went to high school together, and we've gone out together off and on ever since. He's actually a pretty nice guy, even though he likes to do a little rough-housing now and then."

Pete, feeling as replete as Ichabod Crane at the Van Tassel table, thought of the Headless Horseman of Sleepy Hollow. "He seems to like to make fun of people quite a bit."

"Oh, that's just the way he is. He never means any harm with it."

"Does anyone ever take him the wrong way, and think he does mean harm?"

"I guess so, from time to time, but he doesn't let it bother him."

"That's nice to know."

"Are you worried that maybe he'll want to give you a bad time?"

"Not particularly. He seems to like me O.K."

"He likes most people. You couldn't say he has a mean streak in him."

The more Pete learned about Randy and about Nancy's attitude towards the cowboy, the less he wanted to talk about himself or anything close. He continued to ask questions about the town, the farming community, the climate, and so forth. The light conversation wore away a good hour after dinner, and they moved to the living room. Pete wasn't sure what to expect, and he only half expected what followed, which was about an a half-hour of cordial spooning, until Pete thought it was time to go home. And so he left. As he drove home, he formed two significant convictions. For one, Nancy had a pleasant way of kissing; and for another, she had a too-tolerant approval of Randy. The two thoughts did not rest compatibly in his mind.

The night was warm and starry, nevertheless, and far too fine a night to be ruined by unpleasant thoughts. After he pulled into his own yard, he didn't feel like going inside and turning on the lights. For a while, as he listened to his engine cool down, he took in the smell of alfalfa curing in the neighboring fields. The idea of going to see his lambs in the moonlight appealed to his lulled senses, so he went out back to take a look at them.

Ten yards from the pen, he knew something was wrong. The lambs, which usually lay with their feet tucked under them, were sprawled on their sides with their legs sticking straight out. Neither of them stirred at his greeting, nor at his facsimile "baaaaa." As he entered the pen he could see, in the moonlight, tufts of wool here and there. Leaning closer to the two bodies, he could see dark stains on the wool around their necks. The stains were inky in the moonlight, and Pete knew in a flash that both lambs had had their necks ripped open. His search around the inside of the fence turned up no signs of digging under or breaking through the wire, and he knew that no average dog would have jumped the fence both ways. With little further thought, he imagined whose dog might have done the work, and how the dog might have gotten in.

Inside the house, he returned to the whiskey he had so cheerfully left behind earlier in the evening. The light from the kitchen poured into the living room on one side, and the moonlight flowed in from the window on the other. The sonofabitch must have seen his car at Nancy's. *Like to pump his guts full of lead.* If she was Randy's girl, why didn't she say so? And why did she press up against him like that? The poker game came back to him, and the day at the auction. Pete could imagine Randy leaning on the gate of the lamb pen, maybe with a beer bottle hanging down, just as he had leaned that day at the auction. Pete could see the cowboy's face as clear as day, arrogant to the point of indifference. *Like to bust that face wide open. Let some sonofabitch push you around, and there's no end to it.*

Pete went to the kitchen and poured another drink, and he returned to sit in the gloom. He saw Nancy's eyelashes again, and the half-sad twinkle that played across her face. Then she was replaced by the taunting face of the cowboy, and Pete knew his own fists wouldn't get much of a chance to work on that face. But he couldn't let the sonofabitch get away with it. And damn! there was fire in her kisses! Randy knew that, too.

* * * * *

The next morning, he buried the bodies and looked for any clues he might have missed the night before. Broad daylight only showed the same facts more coldly; it was time to ride for revenge. At mid-morning, he walked into Jack Neill's hardware store.

Jack was as robust and cheerful as before. "How's our schoolteacher friend doin'?"

"Pretty fair, Jack. And yourself?"

"Can't complain. What can I sell you today?"

"Well, Jack, I was thinking of taking up deer hunting this fall, and I thought I'd get a little rifle to practice with. Shoot rabbits and bottles for a while."

"That's a good idea. Thinkin' of a little .22, or something like that?"

"Is that what you'd suggest?"

"I think so. It'd do fine for varmints or target shooting. You'd want something bigger for bigger game, but you could get a deer rifle later on. Got lots of them, too, of course."

Jack went through his entire selection, explaining all the differences between this model and that. Pete finally settled on a Winchester with a lever action; along with it he received a pamphlet of instructions and two complimentary boxes of shells.

As he was leaving, Jack gave him a warning. "Be sure you always shoot into something solid, like a hay bale or a dirt bank. That thing has a range of a mile. Course it drops a little at that distance."

"Will do, Jack."

"O.K. Have fun with that thing, now. There's a lot of squirrels down at the creek, by the way."

* * * * *

Friday night found Pete at the Alamo again, looking for his man. He sat at the bar by himself, and he drank the usual bar whiskey. By and by Randy came in, and as Pete expected, the cowboy came over to greet him. Pete ordered two drinks for them and invited Randy to sit down.

"How's the schoolteacher these days?"

"Not bad. I got out of the sheepherding business."

"That right?" Randy took a sip of his drink. "Sell 'em? They were kind of small to slaughter already, weren't they?"

"Didn't have to do either. Somebody's dog got in and raised hell with 'em. Killed 'em both."

"By God, there's a lot of dogs around that'll do that, too." Randy pushed his hat back and shook his head.

"I know. That's what Gus told me. So I got me a little rifle in case they give me any more trouble."

"Some people say a rifle is the only cure for a dog that kills livestock. I've had to kill a couple of my own for that." Randy shook his head. "Hate to do it."

"Only thing is, I'm not worth a damn at shooting." Pete paused for a drink, "I was wondering if you could give me a few pointers. You're probably a pretty good shot."

"Well, there's not a hell of a lot to learn. You got to have a good eye and a steady hand. What kind of a gun did you get?"

"Lever action .22, Winchester."

"Good little rifle."

"Yeah, I think so. I was thinkin' maybe you and I could go out and do some shootin' together. What are you doin' tomorrow?"

"I was gonna spray cows, but I should be done by noon."

"Why don't you meet me down at the creek, and bring along a rifle? I'll bring the bottles."

"Yeah . . . I guess I could. Yeah, hell yes, I can make it."

"Where's a good place to meet?"

"How about down at the trestle? There's a good high bank there we can shoot into."

"That would be fine. How about one o'clock?"

"I can probably make it by then."

"Good enough. But don't let me keep you from your poker game." Pete slapped Randy on the shoulder and got up to go to the rest room. When he came back, the cowboy was playing cards. He had his hat off for the moment, and Pete noticed his hair pushed down all around on the sides, with a strip of white along the top of his forehead.

* * * * *

At a little after one the next day, Randy pulled up in his pickup and parked next to Pete's car. He had his rifle in the gun rack and a case of empty bottles in the back. Pete had brought a six-pack of cold beer, and he handed one to Randy. The cowboy looked over the Winchester with Pete and helped him sight it in. He adjusted the sight with his pocket knife, and as he did so, he explained the process to Pete. Together they set up a dozen bottles on a log against the bank, and then they went back to their rifles. Pete hit two bottles out of fifteen shots, and Randy popped off the other ten with thirteen shots.

"God-damn. It looks like I need a lot more practice. Why don't you go set up some more bottles, Randy, and I'll load up the rifles."

Randy hesitated for a second and said, "Sure. Mine loads the same as yours." As Randy bent over the log, Pete slipped half a dozen shells into the Winchester. Randy was being casual and obviously nonchalant about not looking back, so he didn't see Pete taking aim. Pete smiled to himself, and then he buried a bullet in the bank about three feet over Randy's head. The cowboy jerked around. "What the hell do you think you're doin'?" he screamed.

"Sorry about that, Randy. Forgot how the safety worked. I didn't hit you, did I?"

"No, but it was sure as hell a stupid thing to do."

"Well, I'll have to be more careful," Pete hollered back. "Go ahead and set up the rest."

When Randy came back, there was little of the fun-loving cowboy left on his face.

Pete smiled and said, "That scared me as much as it did you. You want to shoot first this time?" He held Randy's rifle out to him.

He never saw the punch coming, but he felt it, solid and square on his left cheekbone. The rifle fell out of his hand as he hit the ground on his right hip and elbow. He looked up and saw the cowboy standing over him, fists clenched at his side. There was no fear in his face, just pure anger.

"You sonofabitch, I ought to knock the livin' hell out of you for that stunt." Pete wasn't sure if he wanted to get up or not, but he did.

"Well, I'll tell you something. I don't wish I would have shot you, but I could have." Randy looked a little puzzled, but just for an instant. Pete looked him square in the face, and he could feel his arms shaking as he doubled up his fists. "You want to hit me again, go ahead and try."

"It wouldn't be much of a fight, and there's not much call for one. I was just teachin' you not to be a fool with a gun."

Pete turned that over in his mind as he unclenched his fists and picked up his hat. "No," he said, "I guess there's not."

There really didn't seem to be much call, after all. What was done was done, and the rest would work out in its own way. He brushed off his hat, wiped his brow with the back of his cuff, and put his hat on. "There's four beers left. Want one?"

"Yeah, I'll take one." Randy's outward friendliness was returning. "My turn to shoot?"

When all the bottles were gone and the full ones were emptied and shot away, the two men ejected the live rounds from their rifles. Randy put his rifle in the rack above his pickup seat and said, "You didn't do too bad for a sheepherder. Shall we go get a beer at the Alamo?"

"Sure. Why not." Pete got into his car and followed Randy through the willows back onto the road and into town.

Chicken on Sunday

With the passing of each county line, Monte gave a yell that was somewhere between a *ya-hoo* and a *whoop*, as he slapped the outside roof of the pickup. He pictured the counties stretching behind him like a flagstone path. At the far end, getting farther away, were four years of classes, exams, and lousy city nights, followed by three years of working for the county, with more city nights. At the near end, getting nearer, was as much as he could put together in his mind to call home.

As he came out of the Benicia hills, he picked up the Sacramento country-western station, with Merle Haggard singing "Shade Tree Fix-It Man."

> *I headed out west out of Arkansas*
> *My hoopy ran fine for a while . . .*

He kept time, drumming on the steering wheel. Solano County. *Yoop!* He stopped for gas and cleaned the windshield. Back on the road it was Ray Price, as Monte went to work on a bag of taco-flavored corn chips.

> *You came back but never meant to stay.*
> *Now I've got—heartaches by the number.*

Then it was Yolo County. *Yoop!* Another chunk behind.

The world was young. Ronald Reagan was governor, Richard Nixon was president, gasoline was thirty-three cents a gallon, and Monte Westfield was going home.

Close to midnight, he drove down the main street of Willow Fork. With the coming of the freeway, the restaurants and gas stations had drifted half a mile westward, but the bars were still downtown. He parked his pickup in front of the Lariat. Inside, as he expected, he saw a couple of guys he had gone to school with. He hadn't expected these two in particular, but there they were.

"Well, I'll be damned. Look who just blew in."

"Hi, Dale. Hi, Larry." He put a quarter on the bar and raised his finger to the barmaid. He remembered her as being around the first year or two of high school. Mavis or Yvonne.

"What brings you back to town, Monte?" Dale asked.

"You come for the wedding?"

"Nah, I got tired of workin' in the city. Who's gettin' married?"

"Who's gettin' married? Man, you *have* been out of town. God-damn Debbie's gettin' married."

"Who to? Danny Silveira?" When Monte thought of Debbie, he thought of Danny and his brand-new '64 red Malibu. That had been the end of things between Debbie and Monte.

"Nope. Some out-of-towner. Got a refrigerator business." Dale sipped his beer.

"No, he doesn't," Larry cut in. "He runs some laundromats."

"I thought he—"

"They had it in the god-damn paper when she got engaged. He runs a bunch of laundromats in Modesto."

"Anyway, he's got money." Dale sipped his beer again and reached for the dice cups. "Shake you for the music, Monte."

"Two bits or four?"

"Two. That'll give us five songs. Let someone else put in after that."

When Monte lost the game of horse, Dale took the quarter and strolled to the jukebox. Larry took up the conversation.

"You just make it to town, eh, Monte?"

"Yep. Didn't have anywhere else to go, and figured I could get a job here."

"There's work around here, for whoever wants it. Better'n last year. You stayin' at your uncle's?"

"Maybe for a day or two. Mainly to pick up some stuff. Where you guys working?"

"We were both workin' at the sugar beet plant, but right now we're drawin' unemployment. Not ready to go back to the fields."

Dale returned to his stool and slid onto it. "There it is," he said. "Sixty-five god-damn dollars a week. But it beats the hell out of hoeing weeds."

"Well, I might be hoeing weeds before the week is out."

"Beats the hell out of bein' broke and watchin' quiz shows."

Monte put down a dollar and held up three fingers, and Mavis or Yvonne brought three glasses of draft. He had the distinct feeling that he was home.

* * * * *

The visit with Uncle Kenny was short and sweet. Monte stayed two nights, long enough to be polite. Then he packed up his shotgun, some old clothes, and a box of books and keepsakes. He rented a trailer house for twenty-five a week, out at the Shady Grove. It was shady—you could say that much for it. Tucked in amidst a grove of valley oaks, Shady Grove was a cabin-and-trailer court that had a shower room and a little gyppo store. The shower room wasn't nearly as stuffy as the tiny bathroom in the trailer, so Monte showered and shaved there. When Saturday rolled around, he found himself wondering whether to wear a tie to Debbie's wedding.

He knew what kind of a reception Paul Mendez would throw for his daughter. He would do it in the high Portagee fashion, even if the man from Modesto wasn't Portuguese himself. Paul would have a beef killed, and everybody in the county was welcome to come to the fairgrounds for his fill of beef, beer, and that Portagee bread sopped in juice. The paunchy men would stand around with arms crossed and talk about the price of cattle, hay, or milk. The young bloods of town would cluster around the beer keg and tell of their exploits. There might be a wife or two getting impatient with a philandering husband, or the reverse, and there might be a fistfight. In all respects it would be a normal reception. Monte decided to wear a tie to church and take it off before he got to the fairgrounds.

For three years he'd worn a tie to work every day, so that part didn't bother him. It was simply that he hadn't ever worn a tie in town here, except at high school graduation, and now he felt he shouldn't go open-necked to see an old girlfriend marry a laundromat baron.

The wedding and reception were as he had expected—a long Catholic service, and beer well into the night. It held the added feature of bringing Monte into contact with Gary Mauer, who had gone to high school when Monte did and who needed a cat skinner to disc barley stubble. Monday, then, found Monte eating dust and brooding about Saturday night.

It didn't take long for Monte to recall how tractor driving lent itself to dogged patterns of thought. He was disking east and west; at the east end was a green cornfield, and at the west end there was a levee covered with bull thistles. Every time he squeaked the engine around at the levee end, he was revisited by an image of Paul Mendez trussed up almost absurdly in a tuxedo. Every time he pulled it around by the cornfield, he had a recurrent image of Debbie, crow-black hair against a white wedding dress, coming out of the women's room. Alternately, all day long, his mind changed ruts from Paul to Debbie and back.

Both encounters had suggested to him, in different ways, something he was having a hard time putting a finger on. He would work on one for a while and try to break it down, and then it would be time to turn around and start all over again.

Paul had been brief. "A man ought to be happy when his daughter marries well. But y'know, I can't help thinking that you and I missed out on this one." He drank on his beer and said, "Been shootin' any trap lately?" Monte said no, he had just gotten his shotgun back, and he might like to give it a try. Paul said they were shooting on Thursday evenings, and Monte was welcome. That was the long and the short of that conversation—not much, but it left a residue.

The women's room, which adjoined the men's, was off on the edge of the picnic area just before the livestock barns.

"Hello, stranger," she said. "You came back to town just in time." Her hand went to her hair.

"Yeah, I guess I hit it just right. I was surprised to hear you were getting married." After a silence he said, "I wish you well, Debbie. I hope you'll be happy."

"I probably will be. But you make me feel like I ought to apologize or something. I think he and I are more of a kind."

"Let's not run through all that again."

"You're right. I shouldn't bring it up." Her hand went to her hip, and she smoothed the dress along her thigh. She looked at him. "After tonight I'll be another man's wife."

Just for an instant it flashed upon him, at least in the abstract, that she was available. Maybe it was the hand on her thigh that made him think that way, or maybe the half-smile. Her guard was down, and she was the same old Debbie, wanting something she ought to leave alone. He had a fleeting vision of taking a tumble with her, maybe on the straw in the horse barn. Had she smiled more completely, she would have brought the conversation to a more definite point, but she was holding him there with half-smiles and half-statements. The troublesome part was that he wasn't moved, that he didn't kindle to the possibility. So he wished her well again, and he walked into the men's room.

Now, as he pulled the caterpillar around at the end of the field, he tried to put a name on it and couldn't. It wasn't that he didn't have the nerve or bitterness or whatever it took to do it. It would have been a rousing good adventure, something to muse about as time slipped by. But that same inner prompting that told him it might have been possible also told him it didn't matter.

Then he was at the other end again, and Paul was back wanting to shoot trap. In the fall, Monte supposed, Paul would want to hunt pheasants, just like before. Paul always had a couple of shorthairs, plus good connections for hunting in corn and rice stubble. He would get away from the cows for a day and take Monte hunting.

In the past few years of telephones and typewriters and filing cabinets, Monte had recalled the pheasant hunting time and again. Most recently it had been a complete cycle—not just endless trudging and missed shots, but the perfect sequence of point, flush, shoot, and retrieve. They would be on a ditch bank when they got the bird up. Monte and Paul would both shoot, and the bird would tumble into the stubble and disappear, like a rock tossed into a pond. Then the shorthair would be after it— there was only one dog in this memory—and by turns the dog and the rooster would leap up out of the stubble like two different kinds of fish leaping in a lake, the surface golden in the setting sun. Eventually the big fish would win. This was the image that came back to him again today, the exemplary hunt blended by time and reminiscence.

When the hunt had ended on such a day, Paul would want Monte to come for dinner. On Saturdays it had always been roast or chops, and on Sunday it was always chicken. Since Uncle Kenny had not been ceremonious about meals, Monte had eaten at the Mendez table dozens of times, even after Danny

Silveira and his red Malibu had come onto the scene. The hunting was good, and the chicken was good . . . now the tractor brought him to the cornfield again and Debbie, and still there was a sense that there was something missing out of all this and it wasn't just Debbie.

* * * * *

Came the next Saturday, and with it a party at the Costa brothers' ranch. When people had a party in Willow Fork they didn't send out invitations, unless they wanted to keep it small. They just let the word out and it got around, from Chevy to Pontiac to GMC.

The Costa brothers—Billy and Jerry—had both been married in high school but had outgrown it. Now in their late twenties, they were running a dairy and enjoying bachelor life anew, courting the seventeen- and eighteen-year-old girls as if the only things that had changed in ten years were the tops on beer cans and tail lights on cars. Billy and Jerry had let out the word—party at Costa's—and when Monte got there, the quarter-mile driveway was lined with cars and pickups all the way to the road.

Monte unloaded his two six-packs into a tub of ice, and popping a cold Coors, looked around for someone he might know. One other thing had changed. People smoked openly at parties, where a few years earlier, the stonies would cloister in a back bedroom and pass the furtive joint. This evening, the smell wafted across the farm yard as frank and free as drying alfalfa in the summer or burning oak leaves in the fall. As long as nobody kept the younger girls here too late, or set the barn on fire, young Willow Fork would have its merry time.

The faces had changed not in kind but in degree. He saw faces that he must have seen, years earlier, concentrated on the finer maneuvers of skateboards and Sting-ray bicycles. But he did not recognize the face that had gotten older; he saw the face that had stayed the same, grown into by the younger brothers and sisters of the family. He now knew how it could be with the small-town teachers, who would forever be calling Larry by Steve's name, or Linda by Kathy's. In a family of four, perhaps there was a Ken or Judy before or after, so that each would take his turn wearing the family sixteen-year-old face.

Of the many faces he did not recognize at all, there was one that bore an intelligence Monte liked. He met her at the beer tub and offered to open her beer. By now the Costa sound system was pumping out Creedence Clearwater Revival right above their heads, so Monte had to shout his offer and accompany it with a pantomime. When "Cross-Tie Walker" was done, they exchanged introductions. Her name was Kim.

At that point, two young blades swaggered to the beer trough. One, with a rat-brown mop of hair, railed to the other, who sported black sideburns, "You show me a Portagee that drives a Pontiac, and I'll show you a dog named Sam." Kim, for whose benefit the phrase had apparently been turned, said hello to them, and Monte noted that she was blonde. Straw blonde, like barley stubble.

Kim's last name was Cameron, as in Lindsay and Cameron. Funeral directors. Can't wait to meet him, Monte thought. A man who would look at me like Paul Mendez would look at a steer—speculate on the fat around the ribs. Know exactly what my liver looks like.

"Is your dad the undertaker?"

"Oh yeah."

"I think he did some of my family. When I lived here before."

"He's done most families. How long ago?"

"Nine or ten years."

"Have you been gone that long?"

"No. Just six or seven. Off and on. I live here now, though."

"He probably did them. He's coroner now, too."

And so the evening wore on, now dancing, now talking about Willow Fork past and present. Kim was nineteen. Lived with her parents. Had an Irish Setter named Rufus. Her dad was out in the hills, bringing in on horseback a man who had died down in Grindstone Canyon. Said sometimes it was hard to tie a dead man onto a horse. She worked in the business office at Paxton Tractor and Implement. She'd come with some other girls. Who'd left with some other boys. Sure, Monte'd give her a ride home, and no worry. Wouldn't want to tangle with your dad. Oh, he's a nice guy.

At her house, he stopped the pickup. "Don't walk me to the door," she said. The porch light was on.

"No?"

"My mom's dog barks like hell."

That was a new one, Monte thought. The first time he'd walked Debbie to the door and then asked for a kiss, she had said, "My mom would have a cow." She had been only sixteen then, but for years afterward, he had wondered if that was what came of living on a dairy.

"Nothing personal, then," he said.

"Oh, no," Kim assured him. "He's a Pomeranian."

"Then you wouldn't mind my calling?"

"Oh, no. We're in the phone book." She brushed her hair back off her cheekbone and turned to him. As Monte leaned toward her, with his arm on the back of the pickup seat, the porch light glowed behind her head. Closing his eyes, he still saw it, hair as golden as barley stubble in a summer sun.

* * * * *

When the disking was done, there was milo to cultivate, and after that there were beans to cut and rake. As the ten-hour days piled up, Monte sometimes wondered why he had given up his office job. Forty hours a week, air-conditioned office, good pay scale for a college degree. Then he would remember snugging up the necktie every morning, sitting in city buses, and calling his supervisor Doctor Bonner (Ph.D. in public administration), and he would wonder how he had lasted so long without getting sucked in entirely.

Raking beans was night work, and it paid a dime an hour more. It put a cramp in a fellow's night life, but it let him work in the cool of the night and go swimming in the day. His visits with Kim consisted of weekday lunches and weekend afternoon drives. During the week, he would sometimes take Rufus to the creek with him. One day when he did, there were some boys under the bridge where the old highway crossed over. They had b-b guns but they must have run out of b-b's, because they were throwing rocks at the swallow nests under the bridge. Monte was aggravated; it was crude, and it reminded him that he used to do the same thing. Most of the nests were empty by this time of year, so the boys were bringing down mostly crusts of dry mud and feathers. The boys would holler whenever they hit a nest or whenever a rock hit the concrete beam and caromed back at them.

On one hit, Monte heard the thud of the rock breaking through the shell of the nest, followed by the pattering of mud chunks falling in the creek. This time the howl went even higher, and Rufus bounded towards the water. There had been young birds in the nest, and now they were floating downstream, chirping.

"Rufus!" The dog hit the water. "*Rufus!*" The setter took a few paddles into the current and then took a wide arc back. "Damn it, Rufus, get over here!" Monte looked at the two boys, who were on the other side of the creek. "Why don't you guys knock it off? You've had your fun."

"We're not doing anything to you."

"Why don't you leave the birds alone?"

"Most of 'em are gone anyway."

"Why don't you just leave 'em alone?"

The boys were getting sassy, maybe because they were across the creek, and maybe because they had been feeling their power. The one who had been doing the talking said, "Why don't you . . . ." They both started snickering.

"Why don't I what?" Monte expected "mind your own business," which was the most popular phrase, although not the most popular activity, in Willow Fork.

"Why don't you go pound sand in your ass!" They threw a couple of more rocks at the nests, then picked up their b-b guns and went laughing through the willows.

* * * * *

Back at the Lariat, Monte drank a glass of draft to take the edge off his anger. It wasn't the sass that bothered him, and it wasn't the killing itself. A few nights before, he had killed a rat and was actually pleased. He had pulled into the coffee shop on his way to work when a big sewer rat, about the size of a small cat, came up out of the gutter. Monte jumped out of his pickup, ran the rat down, and booted it into the side of a car. Two men sat in a pickup watching. They hollered, "That's it! Run that sonofabitch down! Kill him!" And he did. He booted the rat into the middle of the parking lot, ran over it with his pickup, ordered his cup of coffee to go, and, morally uplifted, went to work.

But a sewer rat was different. A fellow was supposed to kill them. Monte knew that if he told the boys' fathers about the swallows, the fathers would probably tell him, at the mildest, to mind his own business. If the boys had been throwing rocks at somebody's chickens, that would be different. They would get a damned good hiding, as a lesson to leave another man's property alone. But the swallows, they didn't belong to anyone—not any more than the rat did. And didn't Monte like to hunt? Who owned the pheasants? No one—that was what gave him the right to shoot them. He'd heard that line of reasoning enough, and he didn't disagree with it. Still, when he sifted things out, the swallows didn't end up with the rats or the pheasants or the chickens. With the rats and pheasants, he was right in line with the rest of the town, but when it came to the swallows, the town had a coarser mesh on its sifter than he did. As far as the chickens went, he had to admit that he didn't give much of a damn about them.

He was drinking his second beer when Dale and Larry came in. He didn't feel like talking to them about swallows or anything else.

"Hey, Monte," Dale said.

"Hi, Dale. Larry."

"Haven't seen you for a while," Dale continued.

"Been workin' nights. Rakin' beans."

"Mauer?"

"Yeah."

"Not bad."

"Beats the hell out of wearing a necktie every day."

"That's for damn sure." Dale and Larry moved on down the bar.

Monte was well into his fourth beer, and it was close to time to go to work, when Paul Mendez came in.

"I saw your pickup," he said, "and I thought I'd stop in. We're shooting trap tonight. Wondered if you'd like to come out."

"I'd like to, Paul, but I'm workin' tonight. Rakin' beans. But have a beer." Monte held up a finger for the barmaid.

"No, no," Paul said. "I only got a minute. And you got to go to work."

"Yeah, you're right. Maybe next week I'll shoot with you, though. As soon as the beans are done. Week and a half at the most."

"O.K., Monte." Paul sounded a little put off.

"I will, Paul," Monte assured him, "as soon as I go back on days." Their eyes met for just a flicker, and Monte put his hand out. "I'd like to see if I could still hit 'em."

Then Paul was gone and the beer was gone, and Monte stood up off his stool. Hell of a time to go to work. Get some sandwiches to go, and some coffee.

Outside, sundown was heavy in the air. Next to Monte's pickup, at the curb, sat Calvin Hickey's tractor. It was the same red-and-black Massey Ferguson he'd always taken to town. Years before, Calvin had lost his driver's license for good, and when Monte drove through town early on the way to milking cows and saw the tractor at the curb, he knew a card game was still going on. Calvin's tractor brought it home to Monte. If anything had changed or was missing from before, it wasn't the town; it was his relationship to the town. A guy could come home, but it wouldn't be exactly the same. Just some things. As he slid onto the pickup seat, he knew he would stay to see what the town held for him, to see what grew out of what he had come back to. He knew he would keep seeing Kim. He knew that when bean harvest was finished, he would shoot trap with Paul, and later on they would hunt pheasants. The stubble would be golden, but they would miss some birds. And if he saw someone shoot a jackrabbit and leave it lie, he would mind his own business. When the hunt was over, they would stop at a bar and have a couple, leaving the shotguns and shorthairs in Paul's pickup, and some days they would go to the Mendez place for dinner—roast or chops on Saturday, and chicken on Sunday.

Out of the Wagon

Enough moonlight came in through the station wagon windows for Scotty to see the mosquitoes that needed killing. Lying on his back, he could reach out and mash one against the headliner without rising from the mattress. The ceiling, or lid, as it sometimes seemed, was close but not unbearable. Scotty could turn over or sit up as he pleased. It made do for sleeping, but it wasn't much of a house.

He had slept in cars before. It seemed as if everyone had, as if it was a normal thing to do. If he was driving at night and got sleepy, he pulled off to the side of the road and slept. In the '53 Plymouth, he would crawl into the back seat and sleep there. The '54 Oldsmobile had no back seat, just an oily floor, so he slept in the front seat, sometimes with his feet out the window. Once, picking plums for a few days across the valley, he had slept three nights in the Plymouth. But that was the most before this summer. He had been sleeping in the Pontiac wagon for a week now, and he didn't have a clear idea of when he was going to get out of it.

He didn't have to live in his car; he had chosen to. He could have stayed at the labor camp, but there were too many people in too small an area. Each of the little houses had a full family, and the big house was shared by two families, plus the man and his son in one room, plus the porch, which was Scotty's. He got along well enough with Mexicans, better than the Okies did, but one night had been enough. There should have been a joke or two in all of it, at least something to smile about later, but Scotty wasn't looking for jokes right now. He needed to let things empty out, sift and settle. So he was at the river, by himself, on his back, in a shell.

It could be worse. He could be out of money, out of work, without a car, sleeping in the Salvation Army and eating instant mush for breakfast, stealing bologna and cupcakes for lunch. The present arrangement would be for only a while anyway, and picking apricots wasn't bad work to come back to. He needed to stay busy and not run out of money, so he could move on to where the next place would be. That meant mosquitoes whining in his ear.

He was here by choice, twice over. It wasn't Curtis Barrows' fault. The incident with Curtis had monkey-wrenched things, but by itself it hadn't driven Scotty to where he was. And further, he hadn't burned any bridges or had them burned for him.

It had been easy to despise Curtis Barrows, maybe too easy for a teacher. Curtis drove a new pickup to school, smarter students deferred to him, pretty girls acquiesced to him. Yet he was neither bright nor good-looking. He wasn't a star athlete, and he didn't have much of a sense of humor. What he had was position, standing—family money to buy good clothes, family sense to get him clothes that fit, family form to outline his behavior. Curtis was the type that Scotty knew all too well from just a few years back, when he himself was in high school. That was why it was easy to dislike him. From past experience, Scotty even had a title for him: a ruling-class turd.

Scotty liked to call on Curtis, to push him but not too far to spoil the game. And even as he did it, he knew he shouldn't.

"Who's the dictator of Yugoslavia?"

"I don't know."

"What's the capital, then?"

"I have no idea."

"No idea?"

"None at all."

"Have you ever had an idea?"

"I suppose."

Or he could bait him, by playing on the attitudes the student would have adopted from his parents. "What would you do if a Communist came into your yard?"

"Close the door."

"What if he came in the door?"

"I guess I'd shoot him."

"How would you know he was a Communist?"

Then came the day when he pushed it too far. "What language do they speak in Brazil?"

"I don't know?"

"Who knows? Ivonne?"

"Portuguese."

"Very good. That's right. Now, Curtis, why do you think that is?"

"I have no idea."

"None?"

"None at all."

"Well, it's happened before. Ivonne?"

"Because of the explorers."

"Which ones?"

"The ones from Portugal."

"That's right. Now, Curtis, what was the capital of Brazil before it was moved to Brasilia?"

Curtis gave him a sullen, cloudy look. "I don't know."

Scotty could tell that Ivonne wanted to speak up. She liked to have the right answer, and maybe she wanted to help Curtis off the hook. Scotty liked to give her the chance to look good. He said, "Go ahead, Ivonne."

"Rio de Janeiro."

"Very good." Later, Scotty would recognize that his sense of Ivonne's presence at that moment helped him demean the surly young man. He stood by Curtis, looking down on the dull brown head of hair. "You don't seem to be taking much interest in this, Curtis. Maybe a question from history? What was the color of Napoleon's white horse?"

"Go to hell."

"I don't think that's a color."

The young man rose from his seat and landed one good punch on the teacher's jaw. Then, standing, and seeming to realize what he had done, he turned and walked away, toward the door.

"Go ahead, Curtis," the teacher said as he rubbed his jaw. "Come back when you cool off."

The lad may have cooled off, but he didn't come back. The principal suspended him for the remaining month of the school year, and the young man's father came to see the teacher one afternoon after school.

"I'm sorry for what my son did. I thought I taught him better than that."

"That's all right, Mr. Barrows. It was partly my fault. He probably felt I was badgering him."

"I taught him to stand up for himself, but I also taught him to respect his elders. Teachers, too."

"I appreciate your visit."

"You're really not that much older than him."

"No, I'm not. And you know something, Mr. Barrows?"

"No, what?"

"Your son packs a hell of a punch."

The father smiled, as if that was part of what he had taught the boy. "I think you're being a man about it, too," he said, offering his hand.

They shook, and the father left, saying, "Thank you, Mr. Larkin."

"Quite all right, Mr. Barrows."

Scotty turned over on the mattress. No, it wasn't Curtis Barrows' fault. Scotty admitted to himself that it was his own fault—for not having more control, for letting his past resentments goad him into picking on the smug young man. He didn't try to deceive himself on that score, but outwardly he didn't volunteer to take the blame, either. He wasn't in a bad position. The school board had even given the teacher an extra month to decide on signing his contract. Scotty was midway through that extra month. The board was, on behalf of the town, embarrassed that one of theirs might make a person not want to stay. Scotty knew it was up to him to decide, on his own terms, whether he could manage things better if he went back. In the meanwhile, he accepted the board's grace period with a non-committal note of agreement.

Scotty slapped a mosquito against his ear, closed his eyes, and let sleep come to him.

* * * * *

The apricot orchard was a noisy place. Some of the pickers had transistor radios, so there might be two or three stations going at once, with workers joining in now and then. Scotty worked by himself, picking a set of four trees at a time, leap-frogging through the orchard. Sometimes he heard Mexican music and sometimes he heard rock 'n' roll. It didn't matter. It was all background for the creak of his own ladder, the ping and thump of fruit landing in his picking bucket, the soft rattle as he emptied his bucket into a lug box. He leveled off the fruit, pulled out a couple of green leaves, set an empty crate on top of the full one, and dumped in the remaining few apricots. Then he went back up the ladder, between two branches and into the sunlight again, where the sun-blushed apricots hung in clusters.

When he thought of Ivonne Camber, he remembered her shoulder-length blonde hair, flipped up at the ends. Bangs over her eyes, spit-curls on the temples, a little mascara to set off the blue eyes. He remembered the day she was the last one to leave the classroom. The girls had a softball game later that afternoon.

"Good luck in your game, Ivonne. I hope you win."

"Thank you, Mr. Larkin."

"Ivonne?"

She stopped. "Uh-huh?"

"Are you going to the Portagee picnic this weekend?"

She made a face. "Not really. Why?"

"I thought that since you did so well in social studies you might be interested in that kind of thing."

"Not really," she said. "Most of it I remember from the seventh grade."

"Oh." He nodded, as a signal that she could leave. "Good luck in your game."

"Thank you."

He glanced at her tan calves as she left the room. Then, as he sat alone in the classroom, he brought up an image of her pretty face. He realized there had been nothing there. He had thought, once or twice, that there had been a spark or current between them, something on her part to want to shine in his eyes, something in response to his giving her the occasion and the praise. But now he could see there was nothing reciprocal, no registry that he was anything but a teacher. A few days later, he saw her riding in a red Super Sport with a young man he didn't know, a kid maybe two years older than she was. If she recognized Mr. Larkin driving the other way in his station wagon, she didn't show it.

* * * * *

At the river, Scotty cleaned up as he did every day after work. Then he took out his Coleman stove, set it up, and got it going. He opened a can of macaroni, punched a hole in the bottom, blew on the little hole to push the macaroni out in a solid mass like a can of dog food, and set the pan on the stove to heat.

Not far away sat another car at the river, a big hot Dodge that looked like it had been run long and hard. Two men a little older than Scotty sat in the bucket seats, with the doors open, listening to the radio and drinking beer. Their sleeping bags were on the hood, spread out and opened up, and clothes hung in the window next to the back seat. It made him wonder where Morgan was.

He thought of the day he and Morgan cut school to pick oranges. Morgan lived with his old man, who was a drunk, so it seemed natural that Morgan smoked and drank. He might have been a good athlete, but he was already carrying a pack of cigarettes in his pocket when they were freshmen. Scotty lived with his own mother, who was also a drunk, and who had the opposite effect on him. He didn't have the slightest interest in smoking, nor did drinking hold any pull for him. But he and Morgan were friends. When they worked together, if Morgan wanted to stop for a smoke break, Scotty usually stopped with him. On that day they took a break in the early afternoon. Scotty peeled an orange and Morgan lit a cigarette.

Trammel and Cooper, who were working on the next set of trees, took a break, too. They had both quit school already, so it was their way of getting by. Scotty and Morgan were at it for the day, to make some money for the weekend. The four boys sat in the orchard, three of them smoking.

Trammel was explaining how the firemen's ball, which was coming up that weekend, was a good place to get booze. All you had to do was go through the cars in the parking lot. Trammel was tall and narrow, and he leaned forward as he talked, with the cigarette smoke drifting up in front of his close-set eyes. Cooper, who was not very tall and was deathly fat (it was said he wouldn't live to thirty), sat leaning against their orange bin and laughed. He spit off to one side and then giggled. "Like takin' candy from a baby," he said.

Another picker walked through their little gathering, a Mexican in khakis with his cap turned backward, with his picking sack on his left shoulder and his ladder laid horizontally on his right. He stopped and said to Trammel and Cooper, "You boys wan' some peanut butter an' jelly san'wiches?"

They both started laughing. Cooper said, "Yeah, and some of that coffee that tastes like owl piss."

Trammel said, "When did you get out?"

"Just last week."

"Well," Trammel said, "we're all gettin' rich together."

The Mexican laughed and walked on.

"Who was that?" Morgan asked.

"Lalo. You know, the trusty," Trammel said.

"Oh, yeah. I didn't recognize him."

"Who is he?" Scotty asked.

Trammel answered, "Lalo. He was a trusty in jail. He brought all our meals to us."

"Oh. What was he in for?"

"He was the one that was driving when the hitchhiker got killed on the bridge."

"The hitchhiker was riding with him."

"Yeah."

"So he was up for manslaughter. Drunk driving."

"Uh-huh."

"How long was he in there?"

"I think about a year." Trammel looked at Cooper, who nodded.

Later that afternoon, Trammel's sister Betty came out to the orchard with her friend Cookie. They were both skinny, and they seemed to live on cigarettes and Pepsi. They were smoking cigarettes and wanted some money from Trammel.

Whenever Scotty saw Betty, he almost got sick to his stomach. One time he had made out with her, and all he could remember was the watery taste of beer and smoke.

After the girls had pestered Trammel for a while, they stopped at Morgan's ladder. He talked to Cookie for a few seconds and then emptied his picking bag, took it off and draped it on the side of the bin, and told Scotty he'd be back in a little while. Cookie went with him.

Scotty kept working. It was a little after four, and he wanted to fill the bin by dark. Betty stood between his tree and the bin, smoking a cigarette and making small talk.

"Why are you always so serious?"

"I'm not."

"Yes you are."

"I just want to fill the bin."

"I don't mean now. You're always that way."

"I just don't want to have to do this forever."

"Pick oranges?"

"Yeah, all of it."

"What are you going to do?"

"I don't know for sure."

"You're gonna go to college and be a smart ass."

"I might go."

"You think you're too good for all of this, huh?"

"I didn't say that."

"You might as well have."

Morgan came back and told Betty that Cookie was waiting for her.

When she was gone, Scotty said, "I wonder what she was hanging around for."

"Cookie wanted her to."

"Oh."

"But I didn't get anywhere."

* * * * *

The macaroni was warm enough to eat. Scotty shook in some tabasco and salt and pepper, and ate his grub from the pan. He glanced over his shoulder. The two fellows in the Dodge were having a good time. They were like Trammel and Cooper. And Morgan. When those guys weren't in jail, they were having fun.

There wasn't much to do, once he had eaten, cleaned up the few utensils, and packed away the stove and kitchen box. He had a couple of books, but he didn't feel like reading. He had a little money, but he didn't feel like going to town. For the time being, it was all right to be off on his own without much to do.

The world was leaving him alone, even if he felt as if he was in some kind of jail. Scotty knew that this was a time in his life when he should feel free, even though he didn't. At least he knew that much. He thought, if he could push on through, life might open up. He just had to keep from botching it.

He sorted through the box of clothes to get clean underwear and socks for the morning. Looking at himself in the rear view mirror, he decided he would shave the next day. The mosquitoes were starting to come out when the guys in the Dodge pulled their sleeping bags off the car and stuffed them inside. One of them called out, "Ran outa beer." Scotty smiled and nodded back. The Dodge fired up and rumbled out onto the road.

That was all right, too, not to have any interest in alcohol. For all he knew, he might later on, but he was glad it didn't appeal to him now. He had less fun this way, as he saw it, but he had enough things closing him in as it was. He knew that, just as he knew how drinking eventually turned into its own kind of jail. He smiled as he remembered how the Okies said, "Mah momma didn' raise no fool."

At sundown he crawled into his box and lay on his back, hands folded on his chest. It would be a while before he drifted off to sleep, and the mosquitoes would start their whining any minute.

Ivonne was a nice girl, but he was nothing to her and she should be nothing to him. Curtis Barrows was a slug, and there was little to worry about from his direction. It seemed to Scotty that he had come out of it pretty clean, on the surface. But he knew he had let his weaknesses get to him, and he knew he shouldn't sign up for another year until he had a better resistance to the things that got to him.

While he reasoned with himself not to blame a kid, he admitted his own habit of projecting an old unresolved grudge. For the past five years, Scotty had hated Gordon Stanberry, and sometimes he found a place to focus his resentment. He knew he had taken it out on the kid who had then gotten suspended.

It had never made sense that Stanberry should be a bully. That role usually fell to football players or hot-rodders or delinquents, not to smart, well-dressed tennis players who aspired to be lawyers. But somewhere beneath the smartness and the smoothness there lurked an ugliness, and Stanberry brought it out to work on Scotty.

He didn't do the obvious moves, like shove Scotty down a stairway or blindside him in P.E. football. Instead, he might bump Scotty's elbow as he worked on a trig problem, and then say, "Sorry, Thrall."

It was like a knife to the heart. Thrall had been the name of a stepfather, a man who had been married to Scotty's mom. She had made Scotty use the name in the third and fourth grade. Then Thrall had gone to jail for passing bad checks, and Scotty's mom had divorced him. To Scotty it was one of several blights in his life, one he was glad to be outliving if he could, until Stanberry revived it.

"Sorry, Thrall."

"My name isn't Thrall. It's Larkin."

"Oh, I'm sorry. I forgot."

Then came the day in the upstairs hallway of the old main building when, between classes, Stanberry tipped Scotty's books from his hand onto the floor.

"You dropped your books, Thrall."

He could feel the blood rising in his face. He was aware of the stairway and the polished banister behind him, the transom over the closed door that led into the chemistry room in front of him, his books on the floor, and Linda Arneson and Adrienne Wilkes looking on. He was especially aware of Adrienne, the blonde goddess, watching.

"My name isn't Thrall. And you did that on purpose."

"I can't help it if you're clumsy."

Scotty reached out to grab Stanberry's mohair sweater, but his feet went out from under him. He found himself lying on the floor with his books, textbooks wrapped in thick brown waxed paper. Town kids like Stanberry or Adrienne had book covers they bought, glossy covers in the school colors, white and navy blue. Poor kids used grocery bags. Scotty covered his in the waxed sheets they had used in grape harvest. It all ran together—the waxed paper, the walnut stain of the balustrade, the matching wooden frame of the transom, a lime-green mohair sweater, and two blonde-haired girls who seemed to feel sorry for him. Easy to remember, easy to hate—Stanberry had stayed around to be his bugbear and his scapegoat.

Scotty slapped a mosquito against the pillow, and the whining stopped. He let out a long breath and relaxed.

* * * * *

The flame of the Coleman stove burned a clear blue in the dark of morning. Scotty fixed and ate a peanut-butter-and-jelly sandwich as he waited for the water to boil. He could smell the river, neither cool nor warm, in the morning air. As he thought of the day ahead, he recalled the smell of apricots. Always in the summer it had seemed like this, that the smell of the crop was in his nostrils before he ever got to the field.

He had awakened thinking of girls—of the few that had been, and of the ones yet in the future. They were always blonde, all of them, except Connie.

Two years after his helpless crush on Adrienne Wilkes, while he was in college, Connie had come along. She had light brown hair and soft pale breasts. That's how he remembered her—that, and her .22 rifle.

He had met her at the Silver Dollar Fair, danced with her and gotten cozy, and finally talked her into going with him to the place he rented. It was a one-room with kitchenette, bathroom communal, but Connie didn't seem to mind. She was snuggly, and she was the first girl he'd spent the whole night with. It seemed to make up for something he had missed out on. He had weakened with good reason.

As they cuddled, he heard her story, and it was interesting. She was married, but she hadn't been that way for long at all. Her husband, such as he was, had been called up for the draft. The army was drafting guys in their middle twenties, and he knew he was on his way to the jungles and napalm. As Connie told it, he had talked her into getting married so he could have a couple of months of steady sex before he left. She had known in less than a week that there was no romantic love and no patriotic heroism. He worked her sympathy, married her, got what he wanted, and left her with the promise of a military wife's allowance. She was living with her mother.

In the morning when Scotty drove her back to the small town of Reston, she said she would meet him that afternoon along the railroad tracks. She told him she sometimes went out by herself with her rifle, to do some plinking, and she could get away on that pretense.

Scotty hadn't been around guns that much. He had always worked when others went hunting, and he wouldn't have had the money to buy a gun even if he had had an interest in one. So he thought it was curious that Connie would be a gun-toter.

He supposed that somewhere in this set of circumstances there should be a danger, but he couldn't quite locate it in his knowledge that the girl was married. She didn't act as if the marriage was real, and so he didn't feel it was. But when he saw her that afternoon, dressed in a white blouse and cut-off jeans, carrying a rifle, he had a vague sense of danger that was not connected to either the rifle or her being married.

She opened the door of the Plymouth and got in. He must have winced at the rifle, because she smiled and said, "Don't worry. It won't bite you." She set it against the seat, the muzzle pointing at the floorboard.

She gave him directions along country roads and between orchards until they came to a grove of oaks near the river. It was late spring, getting warm, so he parked where there would be shade for a while. Then they kissed, a long moist kiss as they leaned over the rifle.

From the back seat he set her things, one by one, onto the front seat. Once in his movements he looked over the back of the seat and saw her bra, draped over the butt of the rifle stock.

* * * * *

The coffee water was starting to boil, forming pinhead bubbles on the bottom of the aluminum pan. He spooned instant coffee into the thermos and into his coffee cup. Then he poured the water, capped the thermos and rocked it, and stirred the separate cup of coffee. A light foam floated on the surface, and he blew on it before he took his first sip.

He laughed as he remembered a word Connie had used. She was telling him about her mother, who was reading the biology of some movie star. It seemed funny every time he remembered it. He almost ran off with a girl who talked that way. And laughing, he smiled. She had been a kind-hearted person who was stuck in a bad situation, a nice girl all the same.

At nine-thirty, he drank coffee from the thermos. The sounds of the orchard floated in the air—radio music, singing, talking, fruit banging into empty buckets, ladders creaking, a third leg banging against a branch.

Drinking the coffee, he thought again of Connie and those few days back then. He ran into Ken Blosser at the same fair. Ken had hired him to haul hay a couple of years earlier, right after high school. Scotty hadn't ever known Ken, who was about thirty, to have a girlfriend, but he had one that night.

Introducing, he said, "Gloria, this is Scotty Larkin, a kid who worked for me a couple of years ago."

"I'm not a kid any more, Ken."

"Well, O.K. But you were then."

In the rest of the short conversation, Ken mentioned that he had some work coming up, and if Scotty was free, he was welcome to go to work. Scotty said he'd call him in a few days, when school was out.

He went on to meet Connie, spend the night and the next afternoon with her, and come within a small margin of running off with her.

He usually remembered Ken and Connie together, because he met them on the same night and because Ken helped him out of the little mess he had gotten into.

Scotty worked only one day for Ken. In the late afternoon, as he was pulling a bale of hay off the stack above his head, Scotty had a mishap. He had sunk his left hook into the bale and then pulled, to drag the bale down. He was coming up with his right hay hook when the left one broke through the bale. The tip of the hook sliced across the base of his right index finger, opening a pink furrow.

Recalling it, he always remembered how painless it had been to lay open a gash in his own flesh. The doctor said he must have severed a nerve just right, which made sense but did not diminish his wonder at being able to injure himself without feeling it.

So there he was, on the brink of summer vacation, all set to make some money and run off with a girl, and he was out of work. It kept him from going with her. Looking back, he could see it might have made the difference between finishing the last two years of college or not doing it.

He looked at his right hand, already dirty from half a morning's work in the apricot orchard, and he saw the clean pink worm of a scar. Oh, yes, he could have done a lot worse. He could have done himself some real damage, could have seen it coming and been unable to avoid it.

* * * * *

He worked on through the day, with the sun hot on his neck as the straps of the picking bucket pressed against his collar-bone. He finished the day sweaty and tired but in good spirits.

On the way home from work he drove through town. For dinner that evening, he bought pork steak and a pack of frozen baby lima beans, plus a quarter-pound of butter. He drove back to his camping spot on the river, which he had to himself again. He cleaned up at the edge of the river and set out the stove and groceries.

As usual, he fixed his meal on the tailgate. The smell of butter melting over the baby limas made him happy. He realized he was feeling better than he had felt in quite a long while. He could think of Adrienne separate from Stanberry. There had been times when he had wished he had the nerve, or the freedom, to ask Adrienne Wilkes to go out with him. She might have accepted. But she might have given him a pitying look instead. Stanberry was married now, not to Adrienne or anyone from their class. Scotty didn't know where Adrienne was. It probably didn't matter, but it was nice to be able to think of her apart from him. What he needed to do now was to get free of it all—the power that he had allowed those old feelings to hold over him.

He sat on the tailgate with his back to the inside of the station wagon, looking out at the levee and the sky beyond. He was feeling better now. He could tell it was doing him some good to work by himself, keep to himself, and sort things out.

It was hard to think of Stanberry and not to feel hatred. It was hard not to want to beat the enemy and get even. But, he thought, maybe there were other ways, ways to come out ahead instead of get even—simple things like stay out of jail, try to stay on the ladder, and not think with his gonads. Even that much could help. It could help him slough off the past that he had carried wrapped around him. It could make the station wagon seem like what it should be—just the place where he was sleeping for the time being.

Fat Winter

The part he always remembered first was the running—running across the irrigated pastures and hayfields in his tennis shoes, climbing over wobbly barbed-wire fences, sometimes crossing roads and sometimes following them. Always he started the remembrance with running across the wet fields, squilching his new tennis shoes on the late-summer alfalfa stalks. The ground moved under him until he came to a fence, tottered over it, came to another fence and another field, and watched the pasture grass move beneath his splashing feet.

Having remembered that, he would start over and remember it in detail from the beginning, from the point where he had gotten off the school bus and walked into the yard.

No one was home, from the looks of it. Mom and Cathy were still in Oregon with Cathy's grandma, had been there long enough for Cathy to start school. The pickup the old man had gotten was not in the driveway, so he was probably at work. Now that it was bean harvest, sometimes he worked days and sometimes he worked nights.

It was easier to pee in the yard, so Herbie set his books and his lunch bag on the cement steps, then peed on the Bermuda grass. As he was zipping up, he heard a creaking sound from the back yard. Rounding the corner of the house, he saw his father kneeling by the left rear tire of the old Ford station wagon. The man had just pried off the hubcap, and he turned to look up.

The relaxed, disgusted look on his face told the boy that the father was drunk.

"What are you doing, Dad?"

"What's it look like?"

"Changing a tire."

"That's what I'm doing."

"Why?"

"So I can drive the sonofabitch."

"Why don't you drive the pickup?"

"I don't have it any more."

"You don't?"

"Did you see it in the driveway?"

"No."

"Then you can figger I don't have it."

"Why not? What happened to it?"

"They took it back."

"Who did?"

"The finance company."

"They repossessed it?"

"That's exactly what they did, and I'm back to drivin' this sonofabitch." He lit a cigarette. "What are you standin' there for?"

"I saw Mike today. At school."

"Oh, you did." The father spit out tobacco grains from the end of his Pall Mall. "What's he doing?"

"He came back to town to go to school. He's staying at Gellerman's."

"I knew he was back."

"How did you know?"

"I just knew." The father pushed his glasses back onto his nose as he dragged on the cigarette. "What the hell's he doin' at their place?"

"Just staying there."

"Just staying there. Well, that makes me look just fine. Someone else has to take in my kid."

"You told him not to come back."

The cigarette danced, and the spit flew. "I don't care what I told him! You go get him! You tell him he'd better come back here, or I'll send the cops after him. You got that? Don't just stand there! Go get him!"

"Can I go change out of my school clothes?"

"I said go-get-him!" With a backhand swing, he hit the boy square with the hubcap. "Go get him! Don't come back without him!"

Smarting at the elbow and hip, Herbie lit out straight across the country for the Gellerman place. He knew how to pace himself, how to run steady and not get winded. He knew as he ran that he would have to come back one way or the other, that there was futility in even thinking of staying away. Mike had been able to leave—that was a difference between them. Herbie ran, soaking his shoes and spattering his pants, careful not to tear his shoes on the fences.

He turned into the Gellerman driveway just as Chuck Gellerman's car was pulling out. It was a red '55 Ford convertible with Chuck at the wheel and Mike in the shotgun seat. Chuck crunched the car to a stop.

"What are you doin' here, pie?" His pug nose and freckles hadn't changed.

"I need to talk to Mike."

Mike looked across at him. "What about?"

"The old man."

Mike shrugged. "Hop in the back seat. We're going into town."

"My feet are all wet from running across the fields."

"Go ahead and hop in. You're not gonna sweat the small stuff, are you, Chuck?"

Chuck said no, and he waited till Herbie was halfway into the car before he peeled out of the driveway and onto the road.

When Herbie got himself collected and sitting up straight, he watched Mike light a cigarette and blow the smoke into the air stream. "When did you start smoking?"

"Since I been gone."

"Oh."

Chuck looked in the rear-view mirror, "I wouldn't recommend it for you, pie. It'll shorten your wind."

"What does the old man want?"

"He wants you to come home."

"He told me not to ever come back."

"I know, but he wants you home."

"Does he have a pickup now, a Dodge pickup?"

"He did for a while, until today."

"I knew it was him. He passed me on the highway. Wouldn't even give me a ride."

"Shows you how much he cares," Chuck said, flicking his ashes up into the wind.

"Well, he wants you back. He says he'll send the cops after you if you don't."

"Is he drunk?"

"Oh, yeah."

It seemed to Herbie that Mike smoked his cigarette thoughtfully, as if that in itself were a technique that required rather than provided concentration. Mike puffed his cheeks and blew a cloud of smoke over the dashboard.

"I don't know," he said. "It would just start all over again."

"He says you've got to come back. Seems to me you don't have much choice."

"Not legally. I wish he'd make up his mind. He says one thing and then he says another."

"He doesn't care," Chuck cut in. "He just wants to win, that's all."

Mike blew smoke out of his nose. "That's part of it, but not all of it."

Chuck looked in the mirror at Herbie. "Your step-mom and sister still gone?"

"Uh-huh."

Chuck looked at Mike and nodded, as if to say "I told you so."

Mike turned away to spit out at the roadside.

Chuck gloated on. "His first wife left him. His second wife leaves him. You leave him. He can make *you* come back."

Mike snapped his cigarette, half smoked, straight up in the air. Herbie watched it hit the road in back of them, bouncing and sparking, and then he looked at Mike. Maybe the old man was a real prick sometimes, but Mike was his favorite, Mike knew that, and he didn't like someone outside of the family badmouthing the old man.

Chuck went on. "If you go back, he can put you to work again, bring in a little money."

"That's not all," Mike said. "There's more to it. He doesn't want us apart, the three of us. He raised us up to stick together, and here I'm living somewhere else."

As Chuck tipped his ashes in the ashtray, he said, deadpan, "Of course, if you go back, he'll probably sign for you to get a driver's license."

It seemed as if Chuck was being a lot more help than he was intending to be. Herbie was starting to feel better. "Just let me off at the corner," he said. "I'll walk the rest of the way."

When the car stopped, Mike got out and tipped the seat forward for Herbie to get out. He held out his hand, and it was the first time, besides making bets or deals, that Herbie could remember shaking hands with his brother.

* * * * *

Herb sat in the observation level of the lounge car, drinking a can of beer and watching the Nevada desert as it rolled by. It always looked the same, as if it were being played over and over again to the clickety-clack, clickety-clack of the rails. Dark would settle on the desert before long, grey fading to greyer, but he would not need to see the fleeting sagebrush and alkali patches to know that the ground would continue to move beneath him.

He lit a cigarette and thought about Chuck Gellerman. The last time he had seen Chuck, six or seven years back, the small-minded arrogance was still there. Balding and paunchy, Chuck had worked his way up in the packing shed, where he had gone to work when he came back with a string of Gook ears. He drank in the Buckhorn, probably bought skin magazines there and felt up loose women. He could well be in the Buckhorn right now.

There had been another woman, between the first and second wives, that Chuck wouldn't have known as much about on the day that Herbie ran across the fields. She was a heavy-boned woman, not fat, who cooked and cleaned for the boys and slept with the old man when he was still Dad, even behind his back. That was the year before Herbie turned ten.

He and Mike shared a room, slept in the same bed. One night they awoke to their father's voice, which at its lower levels they had learned to sleep through.

"And if that baby is dark-complected, I'll take my gun right into that hospital room and blow your brains out. All over the floor."

Herbie lay still and awake on his back. Mike knew he was awake and nudged him. Herbie nudged back.

"I'm gonna look through that window where they keep the babies, and if that baby has dark skin, I'm gonna get you right here, between the eyes."

"Don't touch me."

"I will if I want. You hear what I say? Right between the eyes."

"Why don't you quiet down before you wake the kids? They're probably awake already."

"Do them good to know what's what."

"Just go to sleep."

"You just remember what I told you. And I won't care what they do to me."

Herbie went to turn over, but Mike stayed him with a hand. The two of them lay there, silent and mortified, for a long while before sleep came back.

Then it was daylight again, and Dottie was waking them up.

At the breakfast table, she had set out two bowls of oatmeal mush. "Your dad left his egg whites for you, Herbie," she said, pushing a plate toward him.

Things were back to normal. Every morning while he slept, she made the man's lunch and cooked his breakfast; then she saw him off to work and tended to the boys. Herbie didn't like eating the egg whites, cold and greasy on the plate his father had used an hour earlier, but at one time he hadn't minded, and now there was no way not to.

On their way to the bus, Herbie asked Mike, "Do you think he would really do it? Shoot her?"

"I don't know."

"Do you think he could kill someone?"

"You never know if he really means some of the things he says."

In the afternoon when they came home from school, the woman was gone, packed up and gone. That was the year Mike learned to cook and Herbie learned to iron their school shirts. It may have been their best time together, just the three of them, even if it didn't seem so good at the time.

Once during that winter, the boys went out to help the father pile brush. The father and a man from Arkansas had pruned the whole orchard, and now they were piling what they had cut off. The boys helped. Valley fog hung wet and cold on every twig, their shoes and pants were soaked up to the knees, and their backs ached from bending over. But it was work, and any work was good work in the winter.

They had lunch together, the boys in the back seat eating bologna sandwiches, the father at the steering wheel eating his own bologna sandwiches, the Arkie sitting in the front seat eating a can of cold spaghetti. The two men discussed the boys, as if for their own benefit.

"Sometimes I think they should have a woman around," the father said, "to do for 'em what their mother wouldn't."

"It don't hurt 'em this way," the Arkie said. "It'll make a better man out of 'em."

That was an idea the old man often came back to, but by the time Herbie was eleven, he had a woman to call Mom and a sister to call Cathy.

* * * * *

Herb reached into the bag that he had stuffed under the seat ahead of him. It was the old kind of traveling bag, the kind Mike called an AWOL bag, and it was full of oranges. They were free in the valley, cheap at this time of the year even for the people who paid for them, but they should be welcome in Grand Junction.

He peeled the orange in one continuous piece, smiling as he did so, remembering how he and Mike would sit on the lower rungs of their ladders, chipping the peel however it came off easily, dropping the pieces in the gouged and bulging mud.

He held the empty hull in his sticky right hand. One-twenty-seven.

When they got to a new tree they set their ladders side by side, then picked the tree clean around till they met on the other side. Every time one of them filled his picking bag, he unsnapped the bottom flap and emptied the bag into the trailer.

"One-twenty-seven," he would say, and the checker would tally it on his clipboard, repeating the number. Between them they averaged more bags a day than most of the men on the crew, and that earned them the right to take a break every couple of hours, eat the nicest orange a kid could find.

Picking oranges was work for an able-bodied man. He got paid by the bag, but he had to keep up with the crew as it took four rows through the orchard—four rows, two on each side of the diesel tracklayer and its two trailers. The boss didn't want kids, but the old man talked him into giving the two boys a try. They would work together on one number, they wouldn't fool around like a lot of these kids would, and by God if they didn't keep up they'd turn in their clippers and bags and stay home.

The boss said O.K. and they were on the crew, two boys working as one man, one-twenty-seven. They kept up. They picked their trees clean, didn't leave any shiners. They didn't pull the oranges but cut them neat and close like they were supposed to.

When a man finished his tree, he could sit at the foot of his ladder and smoke a cigarette. Mike had quit smoking since he came back home, so he and Herbie sat on their ladders, up out of the mud, and ate an orange each. One day they took a break as one-oh-nine took his.

"You kids are keepin' up fine," he said, as he tapped out Bull Durham into his cigarette paper.

Both boys nodded.

"Everyone knows it, too. It's good to see that, you know. Lots of kids don't want to work or don't want to do it right. You kids don't put your sack agin' your hip like these Mexicans do, and try to git by with half a sack, and you don't pull your oranges. You take old Two-Snap, he pulls all of his and everyone knows it, but no one'll say a damn thing. You kids keep up and don't take no short cuts." He licked the cigarette and smoothed the seam, then lit his smoke. "And you don't even have your Daddy on the same crew to keep after you."

"We know how to work," Mike said.

"I reckon you do, and I doubt you go throwin' away your money when you get it."

"No, we pay bills," Mike said.

"Nothin' wrong with that."

One-twenty-seven was Mike's weight class as well. Being lean and strong like their father, neither of them ever had trouble making weight. If they had a wrestling match on a Saturday evening, they got off in the early afternoon for a little rest. That was the old man's compromise. He liked his boys to wrestle, and he was always there to watch, sitting by himself in the middle of the sparsely occupied bleachers. He would sit and fidget through the first three matches, then watch Herbie at one-twenty and Mike at one-twenty-seven. After Mike's match, he would get up and leave, light a cigarette on his way out the door beneath the No Smoking sign, and go downtown for a drink or two. When the boys got out of the shower, he would be waiting to drive them home.

When Herbie went onto the mat, he could always hear Mike's voice hollering, "Keep your head up, Herbie, keep your head up!" The old man didn't holler, but Herbie could feel his eyes on him. When he came off the mat, hot and sweaty, sometimes elated and sometimes demolished, he saw his father in the background. Then it was Mike saying "Good match, Herbie," whether he had won or lost, and Herbie saying "Beat him, Mike." It was always Herbie, sweaty and unwound, and Mike, dry and keyed-up, shaking hands at the edge of the mat.

* * * * *

Herb brushed his teeth and washed his face in the cramped rest room. He combed his hair, silky and silvering on the sides, receding with dignity above the eyebrows. The older cars had rest rooms that a person could move around in, toilets that opened into empty space above the fleeting roadbed. This one was compact, all stainless steel and formica, and it smelled stale and crowded. He was glad to clean up and get out.

With an orange in his jacket pocket, he walked to the lounge car, where he bought a tiny carton of milk, a cup of coffee, and a jumbo oatmeal cookie. He had planned to have a breakfast here, but the booths were taken up and the car seemed crowded, full of waiting customers, cigarette smoke, overflowing trash bags, and stacks of boxed supplies for the tiny service area. He took his provisions back to his own car, to the seat where he had slept through the night. Using the fold-down plastic table attached to the seat ahead of him, he laid out his breakfast.

As he peeled the orange, it emitted a small cloud of citric mist. He hoped Sharon would appreciate the oranges. Mike's assurances had seemed almost forced, as if Sharon was going along with something she would just as soon avoid. But Mike said yes, come and stay as long as you want, you can have a whole corner of the basement to yourself, we have plenty of room. That was what Herb needed, was why he had called. Mike knew that. Herb wasn't sure of what Sharon really thought about it, but he hoped she would like the oranges.

The morning was clear and cold outside as the train crawled up the mountains from Utah toward Colorado. The distant shaggy peaks looked fertile, with green-black timber growing out of red earth and white snow. The land seemed full of promise, just as yesterday's desert wasteland had seemed empty and anxious. Just perspective, he thought. If he were going the other way, the mountains would seem complicated and the desert would seem open and simple. Going this way, the mountains were Mike and a safe place to sift things out; the desert was a wide stretch between here and what he had gotten out of.

Maybe the old man had felt this way each time things had seemed to be slipping away—when a woman would leave, when Mike left after their argument about his driver's license, when the pickup got repossessed, when Mike left again after their argument about buying a class ring.

"We got to stick together," he would say. "Nobody out there is gonna give us a damn dime." And then he could never hold things together. Even when he forced Mike to come back, it was only so he could drive him away further. Now he was living in a trailer house by himself, still in the valley, still convinced that when you're down they kick you.

Herb finished his breakfast and took the debris to the trash receptacle. Downstairs again, after a trip to the rest room, he stood by the door that had let him on board in Sacramento. Watching through the thick-plated window as the roadbed and cutbanks rolled by, he saw three deer. It looked like a doe, her fawn, and a yearling. Then they were gone.

Back in his seat, he leaned on the arm rest. He remembered running across the fields, hoping against fear, pacing himself and not getting tired, knowing it would not last even if Mike came back, knowing even then that he would run across the fields all over again, if it came to that.

He hoped Sharon would like the oranges. It hadn't been necessary to tell Mike how he felt, how he had just run out of fight for a while. Mike still had his own wife and house, and he knew his brother needed a place to winter. That was enough.

Feeling well-fed and relaxed, warm from the sun that came through the window, Herb closed his eyes. He had time for a nap before they reached Grand Junction. The train would come to a stop, and he would gather his coat and his suitcase and the bag of oranges. As he stepped down from the train in the bracing high country air, he would look into the waiting crowd till he found the familiar face. Then, baggage all in his left hand as he held out his right, he would walk forward to shake hands with his brother.

One Other Gaudy Night

We killed the pig on Tuesday. Ron had wanted to have the party on Labor Day, the day before, but the contractor was true to his kind and didn't have the pool done in time. So Ron postponed his party for a week, and we spent Labor Day weekend at the lake. It was a bigger item with Ron to get his boat into the water on Memorial Day than it was to get some skiing done on the last big weekend of the summer, but he was happy to haul out the motorhome and boat to do it big for the weekend. I don't ski much, never did, so I did the barbecuing as usual.

On the Tuesday after Labor Day, I gassed up the old pickup, the one with a box bed and stock racks, and we headed for the auction. On the way out, we waved to Juan, who was riding the four-wheeler and checking sprinkler lines. Juan was good with the sprinklers. He never missed any trees, he got all the hoses coiled up before he mowed weeds, and he was right there with the glue can and fittings whenever the slightest leak started. Juan was good with all the machinery, too—Ron would be the first to admit that Juan pretty much ran the place.

The pigs usually went through the sale ring at about ten, and we made it to the auction in time for them. It was hot and dry already, and the mixture of dust, sawdust, and manure burned into my sinuses. I hoped we'd get out of there right away, but we had to wait quite a while for a pig of the right size to come through by itself. Most of them sold in groups, lots anywhere from four or six to thirty, and Ron wanted only one for the time being. At a little after noon, a pig about ninety or a hundred pounds came through by himself, and the auctioneer sold him by the head. Ron held the bid and probably paid a few dollars too much for him, might even have been bidding against the owner, but he didn't give a damn about a couple of bucks when he set his mind on the pig he wanted for his party. So he paid seventy dollars for the pig, got the pig into the back of the pickup, and we were in business.

We stopped and bought some hamburgers and beer and drove back to the place to have lunch. The contractor's men had just arrived for the day and were beginning to work when we sat down. The pig started to raise hell in the back of the pickup, pushing his nose under the wooden tailgate and trying to get out. So before we broke open our lunch, Ron went into the house and brought out his .22 magnum, loaded it, and set it on the picnic table. As we were getting into our hamburgers, that headstrong little pig managed to push up the back panel, and he was halfway onto the driveway when I grabbed him by the hind leg. I got hold of the other leg and held him, wheelbarrow-like, till Ron came over and put him away. After I cut the little porker's throat, we washed our hands and went back to finish lunch.

I skinned the pig and did a pretty fair job of it, leaving a layer of fat that would sizzle real nice on the spit.

* * * * *

Come Saturday morning, everything was fresh and new for the party. Ron had had the house painted earlier in the summer, and the pillars on the front porch were shining in the morning sun. The pool and the poolside furniture were all new and spotless. Juan mowed the lawn on his new riding mower, and the smell of fresh-cut grass mingled with the sharp smell of chlorine in the morning air.

I looked around. The place was empty. By 4:00 in the afternoon, it would be swarming with people, young good-looking people like Ron, smiling and laughing and drinking, splashing in the new pool, asking the old hand how the pig was doing. I felt young, too, remembering how it was to be young and careless, partying where the party was, certain that the older people had never really known what it was like.

Ron started drinking at 10:00. *That's fine for you*, I thought. I've done it all—drink early, drink late, drink till dawn, drink around the clock. It was still new and brave to him. I would wait till the afternoon, so I wouldn't be too drunk to carve the meat.

By 4:00 the place was crawling with people. There were young men in baggy white pants and loose cotton shirts, with sunglasses and mustaches and razor-cut hair. Ron introduced me as his "right-hand man," and they smiled and shook my hand and treated me like, sure, I was one of the gang, which told me I wasn't. There were young women, most of them with firm butts and trim figures, good suntans, expensive sunglasses, and cigarettes. Nearly all of the girls smoked. Some of them looked at me, not for very long or with much interest.

There was plenty to drink. Ron had set out half a dozen bottles of hard liquor and had that much more on reserve, plus he had had me ice down four cases of bottled beer, mixed brands, in a couple of wash tubs. On top of that, everyone brought something. No one brought food because Ron was having the hors d'oeuvres and salads catered—cheap, he told me—so everyone brought a bottle of wine or liquor and set it on the biggest picnic table. Everyone started with a drink and a paper plate of hors d'oeuvres.

The party flowed on. The stereo blared these people's music. The young men laughed at their own jokes as they re-enacted comedy routines and scenes from recent movies. The motor turning the pig whined in an undertone, as the smoke and aroma of a pig roasting on coals floated through the gathering. The clank of a bottle tossed into the garbage mixed with the smell of suntan lotion, a whiff of whiskey, the thump of the diving board and then a splash, a spray of chlorine smell and the perfume of a young woman walking by, her skin suntanned between the straps of her summer shirt. As the shadows lengthened, sandals and sunglasses joined the purses and paper plates, to decorate the lawn and pool deck wherever there were chairs.

At about sunset, we took the pig off the spit. I carved it, hot and hurried work, while a young woman named Glenda stacked the meat on paper plates for the grub line. People watched, swiping morsels and telling me what a great job I had done and was doing. There was plenty of pork for everyone, and lots of it got wasted—large portions half-eaten and abandoned, lodged against servings of macaroni and potato salad, one plate smashed on top of another in the garbage cans, paper napkins smeared in between, plastic forks sticking out. Plenty for everyone, plenty tossed out, and some left over, mainly shank and shoulder and rib. It was a mess, a beautiful party, with all the handsome well-kept people, their faces shiny now, acting as if they ate like this every day. Maybe they did.

By now I was getting golden drunk, drunk enough to feel like part of the crowd, drunk enough to forget the lines and veins in my face, the grey in my hair. Ron proposed a toast, "For my right-hand man, master chef." I smiled to the applause, raised my bourbon and soda, and drank.

The next few hours are a blur as I remember them. People left. Others came, who weren't there before. Glenda told me she liked older men. I told her I liked all women. The lights were on in the house, upstairs and downstairs. People were eating the leftover pork and throwing one another into the pool. I remember hitting this one young punk, a grown-up brat I had disliked all afternoon and evening, who grabbed me for the next one to be thrown in. I elbowed him away and punched him in the cheek.

Ron, with a girl leaning on him and both of them soaking wet, said to his friends, "Leave him alone." They left me alone.

* * * * *

I woke up to a scary sound. I was alone in bed, and I heard someone else in the room moaning, "Oh, oh, oh. Oh, Ron." They were doing it, and she was really enjoying it. It made me sick at heart to know I was lying here in bed, too poisoned drunk to move, and he was screwing my wife in the same room. She kept up her oohs and aahs.

Silently I turned over in bed, slowly, trying not to feel movement or make noise. I opened my eyes. On the dresser, just above my eye level, was a computer photograph of two young women. One of them was Glenda. I realized we were at her place, and I had no idea how we had gotten there. Furthermore, I hadn't had a wife for ten years. Ron would have been in junior high then.

The cooing sounds continued, coming from the floor in back of me. I would have to turn all the way over to look, and I didn't want to. I didn't want to see Ron on top of Glenda. I felt sick—sick in my stomach and head from the booze, sick that I was cold and alone while someone did my business, sick of life as I lived it and would have to look at it today.

Then a toilet flushed, and Glenda came into the room and crawled into bed with me. I had my back to her, so I rolled over. Her breath smelled of toothpaste, and I knew mine was rotten. I caressed her butt and then her breasts, and she took my hand away.

"What's the matter?" I whispered.

"Don't you remember?"

"No."

"I told you last night. It's the wrong time of the month."

"I'm sorry."

"It's all right."

I got up and went to the bathroom, where I used my finger to spread toothpaste around my teeth, and where I coughed and gagged but kept myself from puking. On my way back to bed, I saw Ron on the floor with the girl who had been leaning on him the night before. They had finished at about the time Glenda came back into the room, and they looked like they were asleep.

* * * * *

We had coffee around Glenda's little table. The other three seemed to be in better spirits and better condition than I was. It's something I've noticed over the past several years—the hangovers are worse. Ron had had quite a bit more to drink than I had, and he was pretty chipper by comparison. He was marveling at what a magnificent party it had been—which it had—and he was looking forward to the next one, telling how he would do this or that little thing differently.

Ron and the other girl, Tammy, decided to go to the boat races. Glenda had things to do, she said, which was a relief to me. Ron and Tammy drove me out to the place, where they went into the house for a while as I surveyed the trash that was scattered everywhere.

My whole body was sick. I felt as if every cell in it had been saturated, bloated with the beer all afternoon and the whiskey all evening. The few words I had said at Glenda's table seemed strange and distant as I said them, and now, even a small act, like pulling around a patio chair to sit on, didn't seem connected to me. I fought against throwing up. After I sat for a while, I got up and found a can of Seven-Up floating in the ice and slush. I took it back to my chair and drank it. I remembered when I was a boy, my daddy used to buy Seven-Up for me so I wouldn't get carsick. That is, he bought it for me when he bought whiskey for himself, when he took me places in the car. Now I realized I wasn't a boy any more. I was just a sick and lonely drunk, trying not to puke.

When I had emptied the Seven-Up can, I found the empty garbage bags, which no one had bothered with at all, and started picking up cans. I stayed at that for a while, but my mind was drifty, and before long I was sorting out dishes and utensils that needed to be washed. Ron came out, verified that I had everything under control, went back through the house to get Tammy, and was gone in his car.

The morning was just about wasted by now. The sun was high and hot, and I was sweating. Flies were crawling all over the leftovers. I found some sliced pork that someone had wrapped in a plastic bag, probably to take home. Then I found a loaf of French bread that hadn't been opened. I made myself eat. My eyes watered, and my stomach fought, and I knew that what I needed was a beer. I found one.

When I finished my lunch, I found the net and fished the floating plastic drink cup from the pool. As I did so, I saw a beer bottle at the bottom of the pool, standing straight up and unbroken. I fished it out, too, and the doubling over put more dull pressure on my head. I sat down to catch my breath and finish my beer. Then I got up and went back to picking up the mess. I put all the leftover beers together on ice.

It took about four hours altogether to pick up, clean up, put away, and hose down. There were nine bags of garbage, which I hauled to town in the old pickup and threw in a dumpster behind the bank. As I worked, I drank at a modest pace, two beers an hour. I drank the eighth one on the way to town, and I knew there were seven left. That should keep me on a Sunday.

It was a warm day, with no breeze. I sat in the shade of the oak tree and drank at a slow rate. I let my gaze linger on the house, the new pickup, the pool, the barn, the old pickup and machinery, the little trailer I lived in, Juan's house beyond that, and the orchards all around. I hadn't known Ron's folks while they were alive—I just knew who they were and that it was a terrible thing when their car rolled into the canyon—but I was sure they wouldn't approve of how he was managing it all. Really, it was their oak tree, their grand old house, their orchards. I felt guilty, sitting in their shade and drinking up their substance, knowing I was on the payroll just to humor Ron and babysit him when he needed it.

* * * * *

Ron came home shortly before dark. There was one beer left, which he drank right away. He didn't seem drunk, but when he suggested we go to town, he told me I could drive. I did.

The Buckhorn and the Alibi sit diagonally across the alley from one another, so it's common for the night crowd to drift back and forth between the two. We started at the Alibi. At about ten o'clock, when I was getting tired and woozy and not very talkative, Ron bought me another beer and said he was going across the alley to the Buckhorn. I nodded and said okay. I nibbled at the half bottle I had before he bought me the full one, and I must have dozed off, because I came to at a little before eleven and saw I still had a full beer. Thinking I ought to go check on Ron, I drank that beer, not very cold now, as quickly as I could. I wobbled to the door and out into the alley.

I made it to the dumpster just in time. I heaved and heaved. My eyes watered and my nose dribbled, and I saw little circles and dots. I stood in the alley and smoked a cigarette, and when I was dried off and pretty sure I was done heaving, I went to find Ron.

He was having a grand time in the Buckhorn, sitting with a woman at least a few years older. Her name was Shirley. As he introduced us, it occurred to me that she liked men of all ages and tonight she was going for the younger variety. Ron bought me a beer and told stories that were hilarious to him. A guy had left his cigarettes on the bar while he went to dance, and another fellow came up and asked Ron if he could have a cigarette. Ron said sure, shook one out for the stranger and one each for himself and Shirley. Since Ron didn't usually smoke, it was very funny to him. Then he told about the bar phone ringing. Ron reached across the bar and answered it, and a woman asked for Jeff. "I told her Jeff had just left with a fat woman. She said, 'I'm a fat woman too, you little prick. Don't get smart with me.' "

That last line was especially funny to Ron. About every five minutes he'd scowl his face and snap it out. Shirley thought it was funny, too. Both of them would laugh and rock and sway on their stools, then lean into each other to smooch.

Ron also told a joke I had heard before. He told it in the form of a true story about him and me. We had seen a woman in a bar, a woman with very tight pants. I had wondered how she put them on. Finally Ron went over and asked, "How do you get into those pants?" And she said, "You could start by buying me a drink." This type of humor went on for about half an hour, and then Ron asked me to bring the car around.

I drove them back to the place and parked the car in the garage. Sunday night, I thought. How about people who have to go to work sober on Monday morning? There was one beer left in my little refrigerator, so I drank it and smoked a couple of cigarettes before going to the back of the trailer to sleep.

* * * * *

I came to consciousness, sick to the heart again, at about eight in the morning. I felt chained to my bed, but my mouth was dry, and I had to use the toilet. Although the little bathroom was dark, I didn't turn on the light. I didn't want to see myself in the mirror. When I was done, I crawled back into bed but couldn't sleep. I was cold, paralyzed, sodden with alcohol and dread, right where I was at the same time the day before, with another day ahead in which I might sober up or I might not.

As I lay there, I remembered what it had been like for those first two or three years after Valerie left me. I would get drunk any night of the week. Sometimes I stayed home from work, using up my sick leave. Worse, which happened a couple of times, was going to work and then going back home because I didn't want to face anyone. At home, I would hide in my own house with the curtains drawn. I would try to sleep but couldn't. I would drink a beer at mid-morning, hiding in my dark fortress, fearing that the phone might ring. That was the threat, the one thing that could pierce my defenses. Had it rung, I could not have not answered it, and I've never been one to take the phone off the hook. Now in my little trailer, I remembered the loneliness and fear. Things had changed a little: there was no phone now, and there was no real shell for it to penetrate. It was as if the fortress had shrunk as I grew older with my ways; it was as if everyone knew I was in there, even if no one cared. Still I huddled in my bedclothes, feeling the dread as always.

Thinking back on the night before, I remembered throwing up in the dumpster, and I was sad at my own sick life—sad to know how common, how routine it was for me to puke up my guts between one bar and the next. Then I thought of Ron, laughing and swaying on his barstool, thinking it would always be a party. I had looked like him, fifteen years earlier. Now I had a puffy face, with baggy eyes and little broken veins starting to show. In another twenty years, if I kept it up and didn't kill myself, I'd have a brandy nose, a swollen liver, and a shriveled dick. I knew that, and I knew it wouldn't do a bit of good to try to tell Ron.

At a little before ten, I rolled out of bed and got dressed in my work clothes. I drank a quart of tomato juice and stepped outside into the blazing daylight. I knew there were two ways to sober up: cold turkey, or taper off. Cold turkey hurt too much, and I couldn't taper off unless I stayed away from the stuff till quitting time.

I took a field hoe from the barn and went out to the young walnut orchard. I knew what work needed to be done, even if Ron never had me do any of it. More than that, I knew I needed a change. I needed a job that didn't nurture my drinking, a real job to stay sober for. I was still fit to hold down a job and pay my own rent. What I needed was to ease out of here and into something that would help keep me straight.

Ron's car was gone when I went in for lunch. I didn't see him until the middle of the afternoon, when he found me in the young orchard. He was wearing a T-shirt that read, "Life is too short to dance with ugly women."

"Tammy and I and a few friends are going to take the motorhome to the coast for a few days," he said. "Go for some abalone, maybe some deep sea fishing. Thought you might want to go."

I shook my head, then rested on my hoe and looked up at him. "Nah. If you don't mind, I think I'll do more good here."

He nodded and looked down the row I had been hoeing. "You're doing a good job," he said. He patted me on the shoulder like he had done the night before in the Alibi, and he smiled at me. "You ought to give that Shirley a try. Pretty good stuff." He turned to walk off.

"Have a good time," I said.

"See you when I get back."

"You bet," I said, and I knew I lied as I said it. But there are worse lies. I could have lied to myself and said I would never drink again.

Linda Morena

Something about the checkout girl struck clean into him, a bolt of recognition that he thought he could feel with his whole body. It wasn't shock absorption, the way a boxer takes a punch and lets it spread all the way to his toes. It was like a ray of knowledge that flared and then suffused itself. By the time he was seated in his car, hands draped on the steering wheel, he could feel it in his forearms. It was as if he knew the girl.

There hadn't been much to the encounter. She had swept the jogging suit across the counter once, twice, three times, and the electronic eye failed to read the price. As she moved the merchandise across the glass screen on the counter's surface, he saw, without thinking, the glossy black hair, the eyelids and sweeping lashes, the faint dark hair on her upper lip, and then, on the third unsuccessful sweep, a twist to the mouth. She looked up and smiled at Gary, then turned and punched the code numbers into the cash register. As she bagged and stapled the purchase, he saw her name tag—*Christina*. With an *h*. That would mean she was born in this country, maybe even second generation.

As he reconstructed her image, he saw the dark, shoulder-length hair, the clear complexion, the features, the expressions. The rest was a blue smock and a name tag. He couldn't remember her hands. He started the car and drove back to his townhouse. It was a warm day in late summer, and the apartment's interior seemed chilly by contrast. He checked the thermostat and nodded. It just seemed cool, that was all. Gary put together a salad, scooped out a serving of cottage cheese, and sat down for lunch.

The girl couldn't have been older than seventeen. Lupe would be thirty-eight now. She had been seventeen then. The girl Christina could easily be her daughter, a child that came along later. She looked exactly as he remembered Lupe, right down to the thoughtful twist of the mouth and then the smile. Maybe that was why she looked seventeen. She could be older.

* * * * *

Guadalupe Guajardo, oldest of eight children, had worked with her family in the fields. She did a man's work—carrying a ladder, picking the high spots, crawling into the center of the tree and gleaning the strays. She translated for her parents, who came from Michoacán by way of Texas and who had not troubled themselves with English. She kept track of the fruit they picked and the wages they had coming. And she smiled at the row boss.

Gary had kept track of and inspected the trees as they were picked. He punched tickets for boxes picked, and he helped the workers move to their next set of trees. It was not his job to carry ladders, but he did it for people who seemed as if they could use the help. The women and young teenagers, especially, won his admiration for their cheerful perseverance through heat, mud, mosquitoes, and fatigue. He was glad to carry Lupe's ladder.

It had been the summer after his third year of college. He was twenty-one, strong and suntanned. He spoke enough Spanish to get the job of row boss, and he wore a white straw hat so he would look like one. The boss was good to him, gave him extra work when the pickers had gone home and when the pickers had a day off waiting for the fruit to ripen. One Sunday morning, as he was stacking ladders in the barn, he saw her step out of the back door of her family's Quonset, lean over the side of the steps, and spit out a stream of toothpaste and water. She was wearing a dress and heels instead of work clothes. Then she saw him, going from the barn to the flat trailer stacked with ladders, and she covered her mouth as she darted back inside. Gary smiled. He knew the Guajardos as neat, clean people, and he surmised they were all getting ready to go to mass.

A few days later, he carried her ladder to a new set of trees, ahead of the rest of the family.

"Thank you for carrying my ladder," she said. "You don't have to."

"I do it for lots of people. I hope it makes the day go a little easier."

"It does for me. But it's extra work for you. And you work more hours than anyone else."

"A lot of the time I'm just walking from one set to the next, or talking to people like your dad. I can take a break whenever I want."

"My brother Fito says you got it made because you work by the hour."

"Maybe I do. Piece workers make more per hour when they're working, though. I guess it comes out even."

"Sometimes I feel sorry for you, out here still working when we're all cleaned up and taking it easy."

"It's no trouble. The boss gives me plenty of hours."

"Well, it's very nice of you to carry my ladder. You don't have to."

"I like to." He had stood the ladder up by now, and he stood under it, between the rungs and the supporting third leg, with his right hand on a mud-caked step. They were speaking through the rungs.

She patted his hand and said, "Thank you," as she smiled.

She had patted his hand during the last week of apricot season. Between the apricots and the peaches, the Guajardos went away for a week or so to hoe in the open fields. In the meanwhile, he remembered the personal touch, that moment when they were two people and not just the Mexican fruit picker and the Anglo row boss. When the family came back for the peaches, she and Gary were like high school friends, with a comfortable feeling in the air between them.

Through the sunny days that followed, Lupe helped him with his Spanish, which now became even more interesting to him. The language became known to him as a living thing, no longer defined by what he knew of it, but a living, laughing, smiling spirit that must be met on its own terms. There were two words for apricots. Nobody here used the first one in the dictionary. There were two words for peaches, but again, he used the word that went with the thing, here in the world of golden fruit, green trees, workers singing and talking to one another through the treetops. If he went to Spain, he could use those other words. He might have to.

He asked for and learned three different words to describe a pretty girl. She also taught him to describe a fair-haired person like himself and a darker person like herself. The first time they kissed, he whispered to her, *linda morena*. Then he amended it to *morena linda*. Pretty, dark-featured girl. "Either way," she said.

They kissed in the tall weeds at the end of a ripening peach orchard, both of them sweaty from the heat and humidity that was trapped there. Later they kissed in the barn, hurried kisses in mosquito twilight as the noises from the labor camp carried on the heavy night air. After that, they kissed in the front seat of his 1954 Chevy, a car nearly as old as she was, a car with cloth seat covers that itched with peach fuzz.

In the orchard, she was always wrapped up in long-sleeve shirts, loose pants, and a scarf; but in the evenings, when she could steal the time, she came to him in a light cotton dress. Then one evening, in the back seat of the Chevy, the dress came off, and in the dusk the white underthings glared in sharp contrast to her rich, smooth skin, her dark eyes, her dark flowing hair. He kissed the peaks of the white brassiere, and then he whispered, "I don't have anything for protection."

"You don't need any," she whispered, and she drew him to her.

In the next two weeks, they made love as they had kissed before, in such times and places as they could manage, always in frenzy and rarely with leisure. Between their hidden meetings and their open conversations in the orchard, he began to know her. He had called her *linda morena* to compliment her in the words she had taught him, and she had accepted it graciously. When he was away from her and brought up her image, she was dark and pretty. He asked himself, was she more than that? Was she as much an individual as he was, even if she was one of eight children, one drop in a flood of migrants who came and went, a worker whose year was segmented by crops and labor camps rather than semesters and vacations? He practiced pronouncing her name as her image came to him. Lupe. Guadalupe. Guadalupe Guajardo. When he reasoned it out, he knew she was as full and real a person as he was, and still he found himself trying to convince himself of what he knew.

Consumed as he was with thoughts of her, day and night, he knew that some of their attraction must be apparent. Hiding their romance seemed to aggravate his own uncertainty. If they had to hide it, did that mean it wasn't real? If they brought it out into the public eye, would they then see more clearly if it was the real thing or not? When he asked her about going out on an actual date, she said it wouldn't be good to let anyone know they were seeing each other.

"Doesn't your father like me?"

"Of course he does."

"Doesn't he want you going out with a *gringo*?"

"Don't call yourself that."

"Well, with a *gabacho*, then."

"That's not much better, but, no, that's not it."

"Does he think you're too young?"

"He might, but everyone's father wants to think that."

"Then what is it? Tell me."

"Later."

Peach season lasted another three weeks, three weeks of long, hot days and breathless nights interspersed with stolen kisses and furtive rendezvous. He thought maybe it was just going to be a summer romance. Maybe she wanted it that way.

Every peach farmer wanted to be done with harvest by Labor Day, and this year they made it with two days to spare. Some of the families left that afternoon; the Guajardos would leave the next day.

That night she told him. "I'm pregnant."

It jolted him in his very center. "My God! Why did you say we didn't need any protection?" Even as he asked, he had an image of her stomach, swelling slightly as he had seen it last. What a fool, he thought. No interruptions for five weeks, never taking a close look or asking after the first time. It had been easy to duck responsibility, and he had happily done so. Now, his major reaction, the reaction of any young man of that era, was the sense that he was trapped and needed to get out.

She was crying.

"I'm sorry," he said. "I didn't mean to make you cry. But why did you say we didn't need to use anything?"

She shook her head and kept crying.

"Please," he said. "If you did it on purpose just tell me, and I'll try not to be mad."

She shook her head.

"Please."

"It wasn't you."

"What?"

"It wasn't you. It was someone else. Already. From before."

"Before?"

"Before the apricots. When we were in Stockton. Picking cherries."

"Does he know?"

"Yes, but I'll never see him again. I know that."

"Is he—?"

"He's Mexican. But he's just a stupid boy. He wanted to know how he could be sure it was his."

"So he left."

"Everybody left. And tomorrow we leave again."

"And that's why I couldn't ask your father to take you out on a date."

She nodded. "You would be in a lot of trouble."

"Your father doesn't know yet."

"No."

"Just you and me?"

"And Rafael."

"The boy."

"Yes, the boy."

He took a big step. "Do you want me to do anything?"

"Like what?"

"I don't know. I don't know if there's anything I can do to help."

"My family will help me."

"Won't they be mad?"

"Yes, but they will help me. They might send me to Mexico or leave me with my aunt in Texas, but they will take care of me."

"What were you hoping for, with me?"

"You were nice to me. I wanted to know if you would always be nice to me . . . after we . . . you know, did it."

"Was I?"

"You were. And besides, I knew I couldn't get into any more trouble."

"Were you hoping I would be able to help you?"

"I told you, my family will help me. You helped me by being nice."

Back in his room at his parents' house, Gary tossed one way and turned another. The alternatives were clear enough. He could do the noble thing by lifting her out of her predicament and making her an honest married woman. But she was a Mexican, and when it came right to the crunch, she didn't seem a full equal to the Anglo college girls. Besides, he wasn't even the one who had gotten her into trouble. If he married her, he would have an eternally grateful and devoted wife, but it would mean the end of the college girls and maybe college itself. Did he love her? He didn't know. Maybe he could learn to—that's how he had heard it put in other people's cases. Could he walk out on her, after she had trusted him? He didn't know, but he thought he probably could. Did he owe her anything? He felt as if he did, but not as much as the minimum payment would call for. Yes, the alternatives were clear. He could make an offer in the morning, or he could look the other way, and in a day it would all be past.

The next day, he stayed away from the labor camp until the afternoon, and when he pulled in to the barn with a load of ladders, he saw that all the families were gone.

* * * * *

Gary mashed the last few curds of cottage cheese with the tines of his fork. It had been all over in a day, but now, more than twenty years later, he was no more certain than he was then. He knew, he had always known, that he had taken the easy way. The other way might have been nothing but trouble. When he thought of Lupe, he thought of a dark, pretty girl, a seventeen-year-old girl in trouble. But as the years fell away, he had grown into one good thought. She had been a complete person, a person with a real problem and a real family to help her, and she had no doubt lived a full, real life since then.

He closed his eyes and brought out the words he thought were right: *Dorados y verdes son mis recuerdos de aquel verano.* Golden and green are my memories of that distant summer.

As he opened his eyes and looked around his apartment and saw the fabricated appliances, counter tops, carpets, upholstery, and even the synthetic jogging suit with its electronically readable price tag still attached, he knew that the other world, the world of gold and green, tan and white, was a long way away. As for the pretty, dark girl and the pretty Anglo girls, as the choice seemed to be divided at the time—well, one of the latter was receiving monthly settlement payments half a continent away, in Indiana. He had made his choices; he couldn't have them back. But now, with the advantage of retrospect, he wondered how clever he had been and how things might have been otherwise.

* * * * *

Gary went back to the chain discount store time and again, until one day, on a cold and clammy October day, he saw Christina once more. As she rang up his purchase, he made himself say what he had rehearsed.

"Excuse me for mentioning this, I know it sounds dumb, but you remind me of someone I knew. A long time ago."

"Oh, really?"

"Yes, really." He had prepared the question carefully. "Does your family by any chance come from Michoacán?"

"No, both of my parents came here from Sinaloa, when they were little children."

"Well, you must not be related. But you sure look like her."

Christina laughed him off, smiling as she stapled his bag and said, "We all look alike."

Her cheerful brushoff struck him as being both polite and shrewd, as if to say, "Thank you for the attention, but it's all on the surface, and I can't blame you for not knowing any better." It was just right. Had she used sarcasm, it could have been interpreted to mean, "To you I may look like a clone, but I'm not." Instead, she had been gracious to him, a man old enough to be her father.

As Gary walked toward the door, he saw himself reflected, a greying man carrying a plastic bag with a set of dishwasher-safe storage containers inside. The door slid open automatically, erasing his reflection. As he stepped outside, he smiled to himself in appreciation of two things: Christina was a bright girl who probably had a full life outside of the blue smock and checkstand, and he wasn't a half-bad *gabacho* himself if he could take a joke that well.

Maestro Among the Peaches

Donnie sat with his back to a peach tree, watching the maestro settle in for lunch. The older man shoveled out a seat and back rest against the ditch bank, washed his hands in the ditch water, dried them on the chest of his shirt, and sat down in his earthen chair. He took off his straw hat and set it on the ground, upside down, and he pulled his lunch box toward him.

The maestro was always interesting to watch, this man who had started out in the fields and had come back to them, this man who gave a studied look to the setting of an irrigation canvas or to the contents of his lunch pail. To Donnie it seemed as if it were the same look he had given to poems and books in various languages—a careful, attentive gaze through the rectangular, metal-framed glasses.

Every day he set the apple and the packaged fruit pie in the lid of the lunch pail, ate one sandwich and then another, ate the apple, unwrapped and ate the fruit pie, and lit a cigarette. Today the maestro had bologna sandwiches and a berry pie.

Donnie liked to watch him, and he liked to listen to him. The maestro liked to talk. Whenever he worked with the Mexicans, he rattled on and on with them. It was the Mexicans who had given him his nickname, which he seemed to like well enough. He talked with them, laughed back and forth with them, sang their songs. Then he told Donnie their stories—about Ramona, the black woman who dealt cards; about Antonio, whose pecker was the center of the world and who reportedly even used it to knock on the door; about Gavilán, the chicken hawk, who danced with all the young girls and was determined to marry a sixteen-year-old virgin; about the old gringo Yeemee, whose wife Celestina, or Sally, as Jimmy called her, had married him so she could come to this country. He had his own stories as well.

The maestro drew his shirtsleeve across his forehead and bit into his first sandwich. Donnie thought of the wet patch he had seen on the back of the older man's shirt as he scraped at the ditchbank. He didn't care about getting sweaty or dirty once he was working, this man who wore a tweed jacket on cool mornings, smoothed it and laid it out straight on the pickup seat when they got to the orchard.

"Gonna get hot and stay hot," he said. "You know that?"

Donnie pulled apart a fried chicken wing. "Oh, yeah. It's here to stay."

"Time like this, you think about how nice it is over on the coast."

"Oh, yeah." Donnie could tell the maestro was moving into a story.

"June fifteenth, they'd be picking blackberries now."

The maestro seemed to have worked in every crop under the sun, years ago, before Donnie was born, and there were a dozen stories for every crop.

Donnie gave him the go-ahead. "Uh-huh."

"We camped for a whole month one summer, right there at the berry fields."

"In a labor camp?"

"Nah. Just in a station wagon. My dad, my two brothers, and I. It's like a different world there, coming out of this valley heat. Got damp and chilly at night. You leave a shirt out overnight, or a pair of socks, and you couldn't wear it in the morning. Easy weather, easy work. Picking berries was like a vacation. Light work, but didn't pay worth a damn. We were lucky to average a dollar an hour. We'd make maybe thirty dollars a day, the four of us. But this was damn near thirty years ago."

"I see."

"It comes back to you, though, when you get to thinking about it. Stray parts. There was another old guy camped there. Boy, I haven't thought of him in a long time. Blevins, that was his name. Yeah. He lived in an old, I mean old, panel delivery truck. It was everything he had, right in there. It couldn't have been much, because he had a wood stove in there, too, as I remember. He was a funny old coot, cheerful as all hell, gettin' by on six or seven dollars a day. I think he was damn near seventy, and he talked funny because all his teeth were gone. He was from Texas, and he talked a lot."

"Uh-huh."

"He was a character, for sure. I haven't thought of him in a long time. Every time I think of him, though, I remember something he told my dad, in front of us boys. Can't think of one without the other."

Donnie looked at the maestro to show he was listening.

"The old codger was having a hard time with takin' a leak, and my old man was always interested in people's medical complications, so he listened to all the details—about running water on the head of his peener, fainting after getting up in the middle of the night, and all of that. One time the old man, this Blevins, says, 'All a young man cares about is a piece of ass. A middle-aged man wants a good meal. And an old man, he's got his mind set on a good shit. Except me. I can shit like a goose, but I sure wish I could piss.' "

Donnie nodded. He could see that he was the young man, and the maestro was now the middle-aged man.

The maestro shrugged. "For a long time I thought he was right. That is, I thought life was going to change as it went along."

"It doesn't?"

"It does and it doesn't. Young men have to worry about food, and middle-aged men have to worry about pussy. That much I know, and I'm sure there's more to it all than just the three separate steps he laid out. I know it's not one step at a time, by itself. But in a way he was right. People do have their preoccupations. He was caught up in his problems with pissing. Other than that, he didn't worry about anything. He probably died in that old black truck."

Donnie wrapped the chicken bones in the aluminum foil and unwrapped the biscuits Julie had packed for him. "Just you and your dad and brothers?"

"That was it." The maestro ate the rest of his first sandwich.

Donnie opened a small can of peaches and dunked a half-eaten biscuit into the juice.

The maestro unwrapped his second sandwich, took a look at it, and bit into it. He drew a deep breath and exhaled, and then he said, "Well, I'll tell another story that's kind of related."

Donnie nodded and took a sip of peach juice.

"One fall my dad was off driving truck in the rice harvest, I think, or maybe he was working at the prune dehydrator. Anyway, my brothers and I went out to pick olives for the weekend. Now that's slow work."

"I imagine."

"Well, my older brother and I were working on the ladders, and our younger brother was on the ground, picking bottoms and running errands. He was about fourteen, and small for his age. He wandered off to the edge of the orchard, to where it met an orange orchard. There were a couple of barnyard ducks waddling through there, so he picked a green orange and nailed one of those ducks broadside. He came back happy as hell with this duck. It was a mallard. None of us had a knife, but we'd had some canned beans for lunch, so he used the tin can lid to cut off the duck's head and feet, and get it all cleaned. Then he built a fire and cooked that duck, all the time calling it an albatross, because he'd just read that poem, *The Rime of the Ancient Mariner*, in school. It was a tough duck, especially cooked that way, but we took an afternoon break and ate it. He was tickled as hell. Said he nailed it on the first throw."

"Are both your brothers still alive?"

"Oh, yeah."

"And no one said anything about the duck? You didn't get caught?"

"Well, we thought we were busted at one point. When we were back on our ladders, the football coach came through the orchard. We thought, oh, shit, but as it turned out, he was just cutting through the orchard to get back to his place. He'd been hunting pheasants, so this must have been November. I've remembered him lots of times—he seemed like a man of leisure, while we were scraping just to make a few dollars for groceries. He looked like a Greek god. You might have known him. He died just a while back. Ray Matson."

"Oh, yeah. I heard he used to be a coach."

"Used to be. And a pretty good one. He would've been about thirty-five then. O.K. That was twenty-eight years ago, and the paper said he was sixty-four. That's about right. Yeah, he was a good coach. They said he could have gone on and coached college. But he got his tit in the wringer, messing around with one of the girls—a sophomore, no less—and he got his ass fired and his wife left him and he went to work at the olive plant. Last time I saw him, which was several years ago, he was driving forklift."

"He didn't say anything about the duck, that day in the orchard."

"No, he just asked my older brother if he was going to go out for track, and my brother said no, and that was it."

"Well, O.K., then. What's it have to do with the other story? Is it just because he's dead?"

"Oh, no. You see, he was coming into that age where he should be worrying about his meals, according to the old man's theory, but here he was still sniffin' after the teen-age girls. And my brothers and I, we had to think about food."

"Oh."

The maestro finished his lunch and lit a cigarette. "Not to speak ill of the dead," he said, "but fellows like that give the profession a bad name." He made a "tut-tut-tut" sound and then said, "A sophomore." He drew his leg up toward him so he could lean his elbow on his knee as he smiled. "You know," he said, "everyone thinks that that's all teachers do, is drool over the girls and give 'em *A*'s. But it was just this guy's hang-up."

Donnie smiled. "It *is* nice to have the scenery, isn't it?"

"Oh, sure. But people see one example blown up like that, and they think that's all there is to it. I think college teachers get the worst rap of all."

"Really?"

"Oh, yeah. These other people think it's a big swap meet. 'An *A* for a lay,' and all that."

"Oh, yeah, I've heard that."

"Hell, I was in that racket for twenty years, and I knew of only one guy who did that. And he was a complete fool."

"So they don't really do that, huh?"

"Hell, no." The maestro inspected the end of his cigarette and tapped the ash. "It would be a sure way to let someone get leverage on you. Make a deal like that, and you're in that person's power."

"So it doesn't happen?"

"Not that way. Oh, there's plenty of diddlin' goes on, always has been, but not on the barter system like people think. It's bad business, and it gets in the way of good sex."

"Hmh."

"And who's going to make the first move? I certainly never would have, not for a deal like that. Oh, I heard stories about co-eds coming in and making leading remarks, but in nearly twenty years, I got propositioned for a grade only once."

"But it did happen." As he spoke, Donnie noted to himself that the maestro was talking only about trading for a grade, not about general diddling.

"Once. And it wasn't a student. It was a student's mother."

Donnie smiled wide, as if to say, let's hear it.

"It was when I was in Nebraska. A little four-year school. There was a basketball player who missed his grade in the class—just missed a *C* by a few points. But a miss is as good as a mile, as I see it, whether you're on the court or in the classroom. So he gets his grades over Christmas break, and he calls up, calls me up at home, and wants to know what he can do about it. I tell him it's already done, on the books. But he whimpers about how rough it is on him and his parents, and how his scholarship is at stake, so I agree to meet him at my office for a conference."

"Uh-huh."

"Well, he brings his mom. It was right after New Year's. I didn't usually deal with parents, but it was vacation and I sort of liked this kid, so I didn't tell him to leave his mom out of it. Anyway, they show up, and I have his grade all laid out and tabulated on a sheet of paper, like stats."

"Sure."

"They take a look, and it's obvious I'm not going to budge. They find out soon enough I'm not all that impressed that he's got a chance to make all-conference if he can just stay eligible. Then mom asks if I can change the *D* to a *W*, just drop him from the course. I say I could, but I won't. I point out that the refs don't let him take his free throws over, and the game's over when the buzzer sounds."

Donnie nodded.

"About this time, Mom reminds Junior that he was supposed to report to his coach at 2:15. As soon as he's gone, she says, 'Mr. Fairbanks, is there anything I can do to change your mind?'

"I said, 'Do you own a publishing company?'

"She says, 'No, why?'

" 'Well,' I said, 'I have two books kicking around New York, looking for a publisher, and that's what I really need.' She shakes her head. Then I gave it another angle and said, 'Well, I drank pretty heavy for twenty years and have been married and divorced twice. I'm all straightened out now, but I'm over twenty thousand dollars in debt, and I live in a dingy apartment.'

"She says, 'We're not rich.'

"I said, 'I don't know anyone who is. Well, we'll try something else. Here I am over forty years old and haven't had any kids yet. That's something I want, along with getting my books published and my bills paid.'

"'I'm sorry,' she says. 'I can't help you there. I'm probably as old as you are.' I think she was probably a couple of years older, but she was pretty well-kept—maintained the cheerleader figure, you know."

"Oh, yeah."

"You see, she thought I was bargaining with her, but I was just setting her up so she could show her ass and I could make fun of her. She was pissing me off, carrying Junior's paper for him and not getting my point."

"Which was. . . ?"

"That what I wanted was unrelated to what she wanted. I had my urgencies and she had hers."

"Oh."

"Anyway, she thinks I'm bargaining, so she bounces right back and says, 'From the sounds of it, you seem to like women.' Maybe she had heard something, too.

"So I said, 'I do.' I can tell she doesn't know I'm setting her up.

"And she comes right out and says, 'Anything I can do for you there?'

"I said, 'Maybe. I'm all tangled up with a woman who can't get it together to leave her husband.' Which I was, at the time. Big disaster. But I was still playing my game, you see, showing her that we were all focused on our own problems and that most of them couldn't be fixed just like that. Plus, I was stringing her along, so I could have a joke on her. I said, 'Maybe you could talk to this woman for me.'

"She says, 'That's not what I meant.' She acted a little huffy.

"So I said, 'Look, Mrs. Whitmore. I can get laid any day of the week, and I don't have to fix a grade to do it.'

" 'Tell that to your lady friend,' she said, and she got up before I had a chance to tell her the joke about the woman who took her boy shopping for Little League equipment." The maestro pitched his cigarette up and over into the irrigation water.

Donnie laughed. "O.K. I guess we'd better hear it."

"Well, it goes like this. Mom's shopping with little Jason or Justin, trying to get him outfitted for Little League. The salesman gives her the whole sales pitch on a fancy fielder's glove, and then she finds out it costs forty dollars, so she says she'll have to think about it. The salesman cools down a little bit and shows her a middle-priced bat, for ten dollars or so, and she says she'll take it. Then the salesman says, 'Do you want a ball for that bat, ma'am?' And she says, 'No, but I'll blow you for the mitt.'"

Donnie exploded. He couldn't stop laughing. It seemed he was laughing at everything, even the old man dying in the black truck.

The maestro leaned with one elbow on the ground, lit another cigarette, and laughed along with Donnie. His ruddy nose and cheeks seemed even darker than usual as he chuckled. "Yeah," he said, "I was getting her set up just right, and then I spoke my mind a little too soon, and she walked out on me."

"But it really happened?"

"Oh, yeah. Just like I told it to you."

* * * * *

That night after dinner, as Julie washed the dishes, Donnie took another beer from the refrigerator and sat at the nook. He felt Julie watch him as he twisted off the cap.

"The maestro told a funny story at lunch today."

"He tells a lot of stories, doesn't he?" Julie's tone was neutral.

"Yeah. He actually told a bunch of stories today, but this one was pretty funny." Then Donnie told the story about the basketball player's mother, omitting the Little League joke, but it didn't come off very well. When he finished the story, he said, "It was pretty funny the way he told it."

"Oh, it's funny," she said.

Donnie felt he was digging himself in deeper, but he went ahead. "Well, he was actually making a point. He said that everyone's got their own fixations, their own worries."

Julie wrung out the dish cloth. Without looking at Donnie, she said, "He's probably right about that." She shook the rag loose and laid it across the sink divider to dry. She looked up and around. "Why is he working in the fields, anyway?"

"I guess he needs a job. Why?"

"Well, it doesn't seem like he's old enough to retire, and even if he'd gotten some kind of early retirement, I doubt he'd be working in the fields."

Donnie smiled as he thought of words the maestro himself might use. "I think he got his ass bounced out." He took a swig and saw that Julie still wasn't smiling, so he added, "Anyway, I don't think he left on his own. I don't know the whole story, but from what I've gathered from his little comments here and there, I think some of his own fixations, or weaknesses, or whatever, caught up with him."

Julie drew her brows together and nodded. "He went too far. He probably hit bottom."

"Probably something like that." Donnie thought Julie might have more to say, but she didn't. He had the feeling that Julie knew something about the maestro without ever meeting him, and it was clear she didn't care for what she heard about him. As Donnie took another drink, he wondered why a man as smart as the maestro had so many problems and ended up living alone.

Shining in the Spring

For just a moment I had the sensation that I was on my way to Sue's in my '55 Chevy. It was spring time, like it always was in my memories of going to her place. I was actually on my way to Betty's, in a '76 Buick that had some miles on it. I had driven for a long stretch between two big orange orchards, and the perfume of the blossoms had made me giddy. That, and the motion of driving across the valley in the warm spring sun, fooled me for a minute.

It was spring time, young time for a guy not very young any more. When I had passed the two orange orchards, I drove along an alfalfa field, cut and curing in the warm afternoon. Maybe it was the hay smell right after the orange blossoms, and maybe it was the hay by itself, but my mind brought up a clear picture of an alfalfa field—long rows of shining hay bales stretching west in the sun. During my senior year I had worked there in the afternoons and evenings after school, for a little less than a week. It had been late spring then, later than now, hot and not just rich and warm. The field was a good-sized one for this side of the valley, maybe eighty acres. Johnny Silva had the contract for hauling that farmer's hay, and he paid me by the bale to line them. It was a penny or two per bale, I think, but I don't remember. Lining bales was a matter of combining every three rows into one, moving the two outside rows to the middle one. That way, Johnny didn't have to make as many runs up and down the field to get his truck loaded. I do remember he paid me for every bale in the field, not just the ones I actually moved. That's a nice thing to remember.

I checked my watch. I had a few minutes to spare, so I detoured to find the field. As I drove, I remembered how strong and clear the work was. My arms gleamed in the sun, strong arms tanning as they flexed, with dry alfalfa flakes stuck to the rippling muscle. Everything flowed as I worked—arms pulling, legs lifting, never straining or heaving as I pulled and swung and bounced the bales, using my weight against theirs, using the bale's weight to move itself. My leather chaps rumpled as I rolled the bales across my thighs, pushed them off my knees. It was a fine feeling to remember, powerful as a warm machine, always moving the right-hand row to the center, turn at the end of the field, move the other right row to the middle. It was hard work but simple and pure in form: put things in a row, fewer and thicker rows. Bring things into line, set things straight.

At that time, my thoughts had been all about Sue. I had wanted her to see me as I worked, to see my warm iron legs and arms perfect as pistons. I knew she lived less than two miles away. She might drive by. That was a good thought. It kept me in tireless motion, even though she never came.

Driving now in my Buick, I found the field. I hadn't been past it for several years, and I saw it was in wine grapes now, a vineyard complete with irrigation lines and wind machines. It would probably never be an alfalfa field again. It was worth too much an acre. As I stopped and looked at it, all complicated now, I remembered when it was simple, open and shining in the sun, getting simpler as I moved three rows into one.

I put the car into gear and drove on. I hadn't thought about Sue in detail for a long time, and all of a sudden it was there. I remembered another day, earlier that spring, when I went out to help her pick shiners. Shiners are those stray oranges, those one or two to a tree, that the picking crews miss. Late fruit, they hang on the tree maybe an extra month till someone gets around to gleaning them. By then they are so sweet and full you think you could never eat an orange out of a grocery store again. It's slow work, climbing up into the middle of one tree after another and getting your arms scratched up. But it was fun, just the two of us in the orchard, me picking and tossing, she catching and smiling. No hanky-panky—the old man could be anywhere. He was old country, some kind of Hungarian or Austrian, and naturally he treated me like dirt. At the end of the afternoon we had four burlap sacks full of shiners, so he drove us through the orchard to pick up our harvest. I loaded the bags into the back of his old Ford pickup, and he never so much as thanked me. Back at the house, he told her to go get a pair of pruning shears and start cutting the suckers in the olive orchard. He told me I could go home. I didn't even get to kiss her.

What a thing to get all worked up about—but I did. I remember that. Sometimes, in the years that followed, I wished his orchards would get torn out by the roots to make way for a mobile home park, and sometimes I wished her college boyfriend would have gotten drafted before he got a chance to marry her. But when it comes right down to it, all she is now is the girl I didn't marry, just as gone as the two I did.

I drove on to Betty's still feeling for a moment as if I was living in two times at once, and sensing the loss and waste that had gone on in between. Sometimes a feeling strikes deep and clean to the center, and right now I had a strong sense of how much the young and beautiful of back then had been worn out and worn down and nobody gave a damn. Then I made it through the mournful part. I took a deep breath and thought of Betty, who no doubt had her hayfields and orchards too. She still had plenty left in her. That made two of us.

Betty came out the door of her trailer house as I parked in the gravel drive. I got out and opened the car door for her. She looked fresh and trim in her blue jeans and shirt, and her hair was shiny in the sunlight. The few grey hairs were beautiful against the brown.

"Am I late?" I asked.

"Just in time."

We buckled our seat belts, and I drove out onto the road. My arms felt strong as I pressed against the steering wheel. "Ready to howl?" I asked.

"I guess so. I don't know how loud." She smiled, blue eyes clear and shining in the afternoon sun.

As I looked at her it occurred to me, for the first time, that when a guy lined bales he actually did away with the middle row as well, leaving a new one in place of all three.

Line and Water

When he thought of his cousin Brenda, he thought first of a hot summer afternoon when they had walked together—a long, bright, free moment in the sun, the two of them walking straight west, sometimes holding hands and sometimes not, two young people with a clear sense of where they were headed and no notion of what they would do when they got there.

That was Brenda—clear and sunny and clean, dark hair against a white blouse, tan legs against light green shorts, clean white shoes that she scrubbed with a brush in Grandma's laundry sink.

Day after day that summer, she wore a white blouse, a fresh clean one every day. Every morning she was bright and crisp as she sat in the middle of the front seat, Grandma driving, on the way to the orchards.

The shed where they cut apricots, Andy and Brenda, was a low, broad structure—just a tin roof held up by posts. As many as forty people could work there when the fruit was coming in. Grandma knew Mrs. Chavers and asked her if "the kids" could have a job. She drove them to work in the morning and picked them up in the afternoon.

Cutting 'cots was work for women and children. There were no husbands or fathers there, or even grown boys, except Andy. The children ranged from ten to fifteen years old, most of the women from thirty to sixty. Andy was sixteen and Brenda was twenty-four; they worked in the cutting shed with about thirty others, who all knew each other and worked together each summer.

Cutting fruit was easy, clean work. A person started with a full lug box of apricots, and one by one ran a paring knife around the widest circumference, opened the cot, pushed the pit out and into the lug, and set the two halves face-up on the large wooden tray. Since most people cut with their right hands, they worked left side to the tray, moving the left hand from box to tray to box. It was an easy reach to the center of the tray, and sometimes Andy from his side and Brenda from hers would lay fresh open apricot halves side by side in the middle. Then and often during the day their eyes would meet, and Andy grew comfortable with her smile.

Other than lunch time, when they ate the lunch they had packed in the morning, three things broke the monotony of the job. When they had covered a tray completely, they would walk out into the sunlight, each take an end of an empty tray from the stack, and set it on top of the one they had just covered. A larger break came when they had six trays done. They would call out together, "Trays Away!" Mrs. Chavers' two sons, Tom and Ken, would set the full trays, one by one, on a waiting cart with miniature railroad wheels. When it was stacked high enough, it went into a tunnel where the fruit was sulfured, then out the other end to the drying yard, where the trays lay like dominoes, the edge of one propped on its neighbor. Andy liked Trays Away because it was so much fun to call out together with Brenda, just two simple words and then a laugh. As Tom and Ken took away the full trays, Andy and Brenda went to the sink, where the shade lengthened in the afternoon and the water ran in a cool daylong trickle. There they would wash the goo and nectar from their hands, and drink from the white enamel cup that hung from the faucet.

The third way of breaking the monotony was to finish off a whole box of fruit. The signal at this point was to take the empty lug from the two upright crates it had rested on, set it off to one side with the empty pits rattling toward the lowered end, and call out, "Fruit!" Tom or Ken would appear, smiling and muscular, with another fifty pounds of fresh fruit to go where the last lug had rested. Then he would punch the cutter's ticket, which, in the interests of neatness and expediency, most people had safety-pinned to their shirt fronts. Andy felt like a first-grader with his, but he wore it there anyway because Brenda did. Hers looked just fine against her white blouse, like an award.

Except for the sticky hands, which they washed off at Trays Away, it was clean work. It was dull, especially through the drowsy afternoons as the radio prattled and the water trickled, but it was easy—women and children's work, fifty cents a box, six or eight dollars a day for the fastest.

At noon time and at quitting time the pickers came in, sweaty and dirty, especially where the straps of their picking buckets had chafed against collarbones and shoulder blades. From boys Andy's age on up to men in middle-age, they were money-earners. Some of them made twenty dollars a day. Andy thought that if he had more gumption he could ask to go work in the orchard, but he would have to learn the hot, hard work by himself, and he had heard that a kid by himself had a difficult time keeping up with the crew. This way, he was with Brenda all day, and even though they didn't talk about much, it was light and pleasant. Their eyes met, their hands met, their voices joined.

One day the pickers didn't come to work. They had a day off to wait for the fruit to ripen. That meant the cutting shed would run out of fruit early. Everyone else seemed to know about it already, except for Andy and Brenda, who just shrugged and kept on slicing. They got one of the last full boxes, which meant that all of the Packards, DeSotos, and Plymouths had packed up and gone by the time they were finished. Brenda asked to use the phone, but there was no answer at Grandma's house. Mrs. Chavers said her boys would probably be done by two or three, and maybe one of them could give a ride.

Brenda looked at Andy. "You feel like walking?"

"Sure."

They ate their lunch underneath Mrs. Chavers' walnut tree, and they started walking. They set out south for half a mile, and then they hit the main road, which would take them due west for six miles. At that point, as they knew, the paved road met the highway, right at the bridge where the highway crossed the creek and continued into town. Miles beyond the highway lay the Coast Range, and beyond that, the ocean.

Andy faced west, held his arms straight out, and touched his fingertips. "The creek and the road are like this. They're about a mile apart where we are right now, but they come together at the bridge." He looked at Brenda's hair and said, "It's like a six-mile bobby pin."

"That's a nice comparison."

"Here," he said. "I'll show you." He held out his hand. She pulled a bobby pin and placed it in his palm. He bent it open.

"See? The ripply part is the creek, and the straight part is the road."

"That's cute."

"And you know what else?"

"Tell me."

"It's how we got to Grandma's house to begin with."

"How's that?"

"I looked us up on the map. You draw a straight line west from Cheyenne to here and another from Albuquerque to here, and it's like an isosceles triangle." He was starting to feel a glow. He was proud of his knowledge, proud that he held her interest.

"Do you always see things that way?"

"Ever since I took geometry."

"Oh."

"Between any three points, you can draw a triangle. Or a triangle exists. Wherever the three points are, they make a plane, and a triangle."

"Even if we're not there anymore."

"The points are. Between any two points there's a line whether you draw it or not."

Brenda smiled. "I knew that. I had geometry." She nodded her head. "That means, before we met here this summer, there was already a line between us, connecting us. There was already a solid line between Albuquerque and Cheyenne."

"Yep. And there is now, too, even though I'm right here and you're right there."

They walked toward the west, toward the distant bridge.

"So," she said, "from now on, wherever you are and wherever I am, there will be a straight line."

"A segment, yeah. There would be anyway, but we're aware of it now."

"Well, that's fun."

"It's pretty simple, really, as long as everything stays in one plane." He looked at her as they walked along, both of them on the paved, empty road. "Are you going back to Albuquerque?"

"I don't know." She winced as she looked at him.

"I don't mean to be personal."

"I know. I just don't know if I can go back to him. We've just had too many troubles." She smiled, a tight smile. "I could tell you more about it some other time. It's a complicated story."

"That's O.K."

"But you're going back to Cheyenne."

"Oh, yeah, as soon as they get it straightened out. I'll probably live with my mom."

"I just thought of something."

"What?"

"You know that big pile of apricot pits?"

"Yeah. Can you believe it? They say they extract some chemical for cancer research."

She glanced his way. "Think about how many pits there must be."

"Millions."

"And how about all the triangles they make, in combination?"

"Wow," he said.

"Andy?"

"Huh?"

"We're two separate points, right?"

"Oh, yeah."

"Even if we touch?"

"Yeah."

"Like this?" She took his hand.

It flooded through him, a wave of everything he felt when their eyes met, their hands met, their voices joined. He felt welded to her, as if a current flowed from her hand to the center of his stomach and on out to the extremities. He squeezed her hand and relaxed. He couldn't answer.

She let go of his hand. "I didn't mean to embarrass you."

"You didn't. I just didn't know what to say."

They walked along, sometimes holding hands and sometimes letting go for a while. After they had walked for about an hour, making small talk, she said, "Between any two points there's a line, right?"

"Sure."

"If one person doesn't know where the other is, or even if one doesn't even know the other? There's still a line, right?"

"Sure, if there's two points. Why?"

"I was just thinking."

"About your husband?"

"No, someone else." She took his hand and then let it go.

"Who?"

"My father."

"Don't you know where he is?"

"Not my real father."

"Your real father?"

"Not my real one. My mom had me before she married your uncle. That's why no one in your mom's family likes my mom."

"I didn't know that."

"Didn't know what? That he's not my real dad?"

"Any of it."

"Hmmm."

"That's a lot."

"I thought you knew it."

"No." They walked along some more, and he said, "Then we're just cousins by marriage."

She nodded.

"That's weird. It doesn't feel any different."

"No, and Grandma's my grandma, no matter what, because that's what she is to me." She took his hand. "I'm sorry I dropped that on you, about my father."

"That's O.K. It just took me by surprise."

"I wonder, you know."

"I guess so. I would, too."

"I thought maybe you knew something."

"I wish I did."

All the time they walked, only three cars passed them. The first was an old Cadillac with a grinning face and a bad muffler, roaring east. The second was a 1958 Chevy which came up quickly behind them, veered into the opposite lane, and passed them with a blast of hot air. The third was a Studebaker pickup coming their way, driven by a farmer with a black cocker spaniel standing in his lap, paws on the window ledge. The farmer waved. Andy and Brenda waved back.

At the bridge, Brenda asked what time he thought it was.

Andy looked at the sun. "Probably about 2:30."

Grandma usually left the house at a little before four.

"Let's go cool off," Brenda said. When they reached the edge of the creek, she slipped off her shoes and stood in the water up to her calves.

Andy took off his shoes and socks, rolled up his pants, and stood next to her in the shade of the bridge. They were almost directly under the bridge, so they could not see the cars that went thumping overhead. Andy looked at his feet, then at hers, then at her calves and the shorts and the blouse and her sweet quiet smile. Their hands met, then their lips, and then it was all a smooth flow of water and shadow, grass and damp sand, soft kisses, light green shorts, lace, moistness around him like he had never felt, and somewhere beyond, outside of himself, the feeling that he had always known it would be this way.

He saw Brenda smiling up at him. "That was nice," she said. "You make me feel good, you know that?"

He didn't know it, but he nodded. He went to push himself up, but she pressed at the small of his back and said, "Not yet." And he stayed there and kissed her, long and sweet. Then she asked, "Are we still two separate points?"

It went against what he had learned in school: that there could not be two points in the same place, that any two points, no matter how close, have distance between them. But geometry had dissolved in that free moment of being more and less than himself, and he said, "No."

Again and again that summer, as he learned how steps in the process went together, as he learned part and method, there remained the magic, the freedom from straight lines and connection, the beauty of losing form and boundary, giving up and letting go.

Most of the time it was at night, when the lights had been out for a while. Then one afternoon, when they had gone to revisit the bridge, he saw the stretch marks. He didn't know what to call them, but at his noticing she said, "Those are stretch marks."

"What from?"

"A woman gets them from being pregnant."

"Have you?"

She nodded.

"You had a baby?"

She nodded.

He shook his head. He knew that a baby was a possible result of all of this, but he couldn't quite connect the idea of a baby with this girl, really, as he saw her.

"Where is it?"

"I don't know."

"You don't know?"

"I gave it up."

"Before you came here?"

"Long before. Before I married Dennis."

Andy stared at her. It seemed as if things were going backward.

"I was pregnant when I met Dennis. He said he would marry me, that he loved me. Then when we were engaged, he said I had to give up the baby."

"And you did."

"It's hard to explain how you feel when you're in trouble. But you feel alone and lost, and you don't see how things could ever be different, and if you see a way out, you take it."

"That's a lot to think about."

"There's a lot more to it, but that's the short version."

"And that's part of the reason you aren't getting along now?"

"That, and other things, but that's part of it." She patted his head. "I know. I just dropped another bomb on you. I'm sorry. But it's not something you can hide from someone you care about."

"Sometimes I feel like a little kid."

"Sometimes. And sometimes not."

* * * * *

Andy answered the phone on the second ring, out of habit. When he got it straight that it was Brenda on the other end, he connected the distant image with the present voice. He could see her as he had seen her then—white blouse, pale green shorts, tan legs, and white shoes. He had known her then as well as he had known anyone up to that point in his life, but now he wasn't sure he knew her at all.

It was like talking through the window in a visiting booth at the county jail. There was something between them. Maybe it was the years. All the time that they talked—as she talked, asked questions, and listened—his mind was on two tracks.

"So are you married?" she asked.

"Not now. I was."

"Kids?"

"One, a girl. Her name's Tiffany. She's fourteen now."

"Does she live with her mom?"

"Yeah. How about yourself?"

"I don't live with my mom."

Andy held his tongue. *You're almost fifty*, he thought. *And your mother's dead.* "O.K. Kids?"

"Two girls. Robin and Michelle. They're both on their own."

"Are you married, or do I dare ask?"

"Married."

"Name of the lucky gentleman?"

"Rick."

"How long have you been with Rick?"

"Nine years."

"Then he's not the father of your girls."

"No, that was Ernie."

"Is Rick listening?"

"He's sitting in the next room. I'm in the kitchen."

"He doesn't care if you mention Ernie, then."

"Oh, no. We all have our pasts."

"Sounds like you did all right, then."

"Keep trying till you get it right."

Empty tennis shoes in the sand. Stretch marks. No, not unless she says something.

". . . since Grandma died. I just think we've been out of touch for too long."

"Oh, yeah. It's been a long time."

"It's like Grandma said, at least the way I see it. I'm part of this family whether people like me or not."

Hands touching, a shimmering road looking west.

". . . and you've always been special to me."

What does Rick. . .

" . . . even if your mom never cared for me."

"I doubt that that matters much now." Mom in a bronze coffin, dry snowflakes on artificial green carpet. Then Uncle Carl, black letters on grey paper, eternal rest and the glory of God, envelope postmarked El Paso, TX. Nothing left between Mom and Brenda.

". . . what your plans are for Christmas. We could drive up between Christmas and New Year, maybe you could meet us somewhere."

"You and Rich."

"Rick."

"Right."

"Maybe you have plans, I don't know."

"I could find time during that week."

"I have to work on him a little more. I don't want to have to drive by myself."

Holiday Inn. Lounge, sunny room, sauna. Pool.

" . . . Salt Lake. That's about half way between Phoenix and your place, isn't it?"

Like a broad-gabled roof. "Probably."

"Does that sound at all possible to you?"

"Oh, yeah." Six hours from Rapid to Cheyenne. Nine more at least to Salt Lake.

"I would really like it. We have a lot of catching up to do."

"It sounds fine to me."

"I'll work on Rick."

"You do that."

"I was just kidding earlier."

"When?"

"When I said I was in the kitchen. I'm actually calling from work."

"Oh."

"I'm sorry. I guess I thought it was funny."

"Maybe it was."

"I'm sorry, Andy. But it really would mean a lot to me if we could get together. There's not much of the family left, really."

"I'd like it, too."

"Really?"

"Really."

"O.K. I'll work on Rick."

"Wherever he is."

"That's right. Wherever he is."

"Shall I wait to hear from you?"

"Why not? It doesn't cost me anything to call from the office. But let me give you both numbers just in case."

Andy cradled the receiver and stared at the arc of numbers and letters that marked off the points on the dial. He had just talked to Brenda, or some version of her. To the extent that he was still Andy, she was still Brenda, the two of them as points that had moved through time and widened the angle. He had thought about her from time to time but never strongly enough to find her out and give a call. But she had felt something strongly enough to call him. She had some reason, formed or unformed, to make the connection.

As he sat there now, by the silent phone, looking past it at the moonlit snow, it seemed important that she had gotten in touch. If she had something on her mind, it mattered to him, too.

He sensed that there was a mixed signal in there somewhere. The call didn't seem to be about the husband named Rick, and it didn't seem to be just about Andy and Brenda. But it was about something, something that made her want to re-trace a line. And whatever it was, it mattered. Their relative geometry might have shifted, but he felt the bond as he always had, a line straight between them. It was a sure connection, the telephone aside.

Thanksgiving came and went. Two more weeks passed. No call, no letter. Then he had a call from Lillian, Brenda's mother's sister. Her voice was pinched and nasal, the way voices sound after too many years of drinking or whining or both.

"She's just up to no good, that's all."

"What's wrong?"

"She's got it into her head that her real father is Tommy Royale."

"Tommy Royale? You mean the famous one? The ballplayer?"

"Yes, the real one."

"Did Audrey know him? Was he even around then?"

"Yes, he was around. That's where Brenda got the idea. He played winter ball down here in the Sun League."

Tommy Royale, dark-eyed Pittsburgh Pirate, left fielder, .300 average, Game of the Week and Aqua Velva. Bluebeard. "Is he still alive?"

"Yes, he is, and he doesn't need to be bothered with this kind of shit."

"Who put her on to this?"

"Who put her on to it? Why, my understanding is that you did."

"Me? This is the first I've ever heard of it."

"Are you sure?"

"Of course I'm sure. Why did you think it was me?"

"Because your mother hated Audrey so bad, that's why."

"Oh, my God. I never heard any of this. Did Audrey even know Tommy Royale?"

"I don't see where any of it is any of your business. And that's why I called you, to ask you to keep your nose out."

"Look, Lillian, this is the first I've heard of it."

"Well, then let's make it the last."

"Fine with me." Click. Bitch. Your sister lies all the way to the grave, and you call me up to chew my ass out.

* * * * *

On the day after Christmas, Andy called Brenda's home number. A man's voice came over the line.

Andy had the name ready. "Hello, Rick? This is Andy, Brenda's cousin. I was wondering if I could speak with her."

"She doesn't want to talk to you."

"Are you sure?"

"Yes, I'm sure."

Andy put the dead receiver in the cradle. Maybe he didn't know her, after all. For all he knew, she might have had the National Enquirer mentality, and called because she thought he knew something about Tommy Royale. After that maybe she'd lost nerve, or her husband had put the kibosh on the idea. Or it might have something to do with the baby she had given up. It was hard to make sense of, with so little to go on. Then again, maybe she didn't have Andy caught up in a search for buried relationships, just wanted to renew old family ties, and the husband didn't like it, for whatever reasons.

It was too bad. She had to be troubled about something, one way or the other, and it seemed there was nothing he could do on his end but wait.

For most of the next two days, Andy brooded about Brenda and what she might be after. It seemed as if she was walled off, and he was sharing her helplessness. Then it came to him that he didn't have to be that way, that he could do something even if she couldn't. He found the work number she had given him, and he called it.

When her voice came over the line, at first she apologized and said she had had a lot of things come up. Then he put it straight: how about if he flew to Phoenix, and they met for lunch?

She said she would like that.

* * * * *

He knew her at once. He noticed the grey in her dark hair, a fullness in her face and figure, and an air of weariness to her whole person, but she was clearly Brenda. She took his hand, and then they kissed each other on the cheek.

The restaurant she had picked for their meeting was what people called a saloon, with plenty of brass, woodwork, ceiling fans, and frosted glass. Andy and Brenda sat at a booth by an interior wall, with its own lamp and fern.

"Rick still hasn't told me that you called," she said.

"It probably doesn't matter."

"He's been pretty hard-headed recently."

"He seemed that way, to me at least."

"Well, I'm sorry."

"You don't have to apologize for him."

"Well, it hasn't helped."

The waitress brought large folding menus, and as Andy and Brenda each looked over the selection, Andy said, "I have to tell you that I talked with your Aunt Lillian, too. She gave me a call."

"I was afraid she might do something like that."

Andy hesitated a second, and then he lowered his menu and asked, "Was there anything that you wanted to ask me about?"

She put her menu on the table, and she nodded. "Yes, there is. A long time ago, I asked you if you knew anything about my father."

"I remember that."

"And you told me you didn't."

"Which was true."

"And I believed you. Well, in the last few months—really, in the last couple of years but even more so in the last few months—I've been wanting to get some of that old stuff cleared up."

"And you thought I might know more than I did then."

"I thought I could ask."

"Well, I suppose you've gathered by now that I still don't know anything."

"I wasn't intending to pump you for information."

"I didn't mean that you were. I guess I was just apologizing for not knowing anything."

"Oh . . ."

"And I guess I was suggesting that I was willing to listen to whatever you might want to ask or tell me."

She smiled at him, and her face softened. "Thank you."

He winked.

"Well," she said, "I imagine Aunt Lillian told you about Tommy Royale."

"Yeah. She thought I was the source of that, um, story."

"No, I heard it through another cousin on my mother's side."

"Did you find out anything more?"

"I was able to find him without too much trouble. He lives in a retirement community near Atlanta. I talked to him on the phone, but not in person."

"What was his response?"

Brenda shook her head. "Stonewalled it all the way."

Andy looked at her hands, which were together and on top of the menu. He met her eyes and asked, "What do you think?"

"I think he's my father. In here—" she pointed to her chest— "I'm sure he is. But he doesn't see any reason to think so, and his lawyer has told him not to talk to me. I think the lawyer has convinced him that I'm trying to get some money."

"That's too bad. Is there anything else you can do?"

"Not really. I don't think there's any more information to dig up, and if someone else really is my dad, I wouldn't know where to begin at this point."

Andy shrugged. "I wish there was something I could do, but I can't think of anything. I think it's a good idea to get this sort of thing out in the open if you can, though."

Brenda nodded. "I think Grandma would have told me what she knew, but it's too late for that now."

The waitress came to take their order. Brenda ordered a chef's salad, and Andy ordered a taco salad. They sipped on their water, and Brenda said, "Andy?"

"Yes?"

"There's another part to this."

"O.K. Go ahead."

"Do you remember that there was another thing I told you, back then?"

"About the baby?"

"Yes."

"Sure, I remember." He hesitated and said, "You said you had given it up."

"Well, I had, and I don't think anyone who has done that just forgets about it. I didn't. All the time my other two girls were growing up, I always wondered what the first one was like, what she was doing, what she looked like."

"It was a girl, too?"

Brenda nodded. "Uh-huh." She took another sip of her water. "But I wanted to know. And after Robin and Michelle were grown up and on their own, I wanted to know more than ever. There was a part of me that was missing, and I just wanted to know, that was all. I didn't want to claim her as my daughter or anything like that."

"You just wanted to know where the line went to."

She looked at him in question, her eyebrows tensed.

"Two points, a line between."

Her face relaxed. "Oh, yes. Exactly. I wanted to know about the other point, and once I knew where the line was drawn, that would have been enough."

"Did you have any luck?"

"I guess you could call it luck. I found out about her."

"And——?"

"Well, it's pretty normal. Her name is Rachel, she's twenty-six—turned twenty-six in September—she's married to a restaurant manager, and they live in Branson, Missouri."

"You haven't met her?"

"No. At first I thought it would be enough just to know about her. Then, of course, once I found out, I wanted to meet her."

"And she didn't want to?"

"I didn't get to ask her. This was right after I got all the resistance from Aunt Lillian and the lawyer, and Rick said it would be just as well to drop everything. He said he was fed up, and what was done was done."

"So he stopped it right there?"

"I guess you could say that."

Andy wrinkled his nose. "It's hard for me to see how you can let him decide that."

"He's good to me about everything else. But he gets pretty short with me about this. He says I should just let sleeping dogs lie, and we should get on with our life together."

"Sort of jealous, then."

"I suppose that's one way of looking at it."

"Did you think I knew anything about—Rachel, is it?—or did you just want to know about the father part?"

"It was all related. It still is. It's like one big puzzle. If I get them figured out, then maybe I'll feel like I know more about myself. Does that make sense?"

"Oh, yeah."

"And I guess I thought that even if you didn't know the facts I was looking for, you knew me, and you'd understand."

"I think I do. At least I'm trying—to understand, you know."

She put her left hand onto the table, and he put his right hand with it. They touched and then released. Her eyes were watering as she said, "I've always felt that you knew me, and you'd understand why I needed to try to get some answers."

"And Rick doesn't understand that, does he?"

"No, not really."

"Well, I'm trying to think of what else I can do to make things better for you. I feel bad, in a way, that you're still in this two-way deadlock, and I can't do anything to change it."

"Just understanding means a lot. And coming all the way here just to have lunch with me and listen to me—that's more than I could have asked."

After they had eaten lunch, Andy paid the bill and walked with Brenda to the sidewalk.

"Thank you for lunch," she said, as she held out her hand.

"Thank you," he said, taking her hand and moving toward her as she moved towards him. Their lips met. He felt as if the years vanished as he and Brenda came together, two points on a warm sidewalk in Phoenix.

In the next moment she was gone, and Andy was reaching in his pocket for the keys of the rental car that would take him back to the airport. He paused for a moment to ponder his mental image of Brenda. It was probably as much as he could have asked for, to know that there was still a line between them, just as they had drawn it that day—that free and bright afternoon when they walked together, on the way to the place where the hot dry road met the water.

Bachelor Trove

"*Morcilla*," Justo said, lisping the Castilian letter *c*.

We were eating blood sausage at a dead man's house. The dead man was Justo's brother, who had made his own *morcilla*, cured his own ham, canned his own tomatoes, and bottled his own wine. Justo and I were trying to enjoy these things. The strong red wine helped.

"*Buen muchacho*," Justo had said. A good boy. That is how he had summed up his younger brother Iñaki, who had died a month earlier of bone cancer. I remembered meeting Iñaki once, ten or twelve years earlier, when their sister Estefanía had come from Spain to visit. Iñaki was slender and quiet and clean. He worked in a bakery and looked pale. That's how I remember him—more like his sister, who was also slender and delicate, than like his brother. Justo was robust, dark-headed like all Basques I had known, heavy-bearded and rosy-cheeked like most of them, and weathered from his work as a gardener.

"*Buen muchacho*," he said of his younger brother, the frail one who didn't tell anyone he was sick until very close to the end. He was forty-seven when he died.

Justo had cut into a new ham, had cut half a dozen slices and fried them in a skillet, then dumped in a quart of tomatoes. In a separate skillet he had cooked the blood sausage. That, and the musky wine, and a loaf of French bread we had brought with us, made our lunch.

When I think of Basques, I think of lamb. A Basque can eat lamb every day, and when he goes to a Basque restaurant, he will order lamb. I've eaten lamb dozens of times over the years that I've visited with Justo, but my best memories are of the blood sausage and red wine, which linger in memory like a rich aftertaste.

After lunch we cleared the table. Having offered to wash the dishes, I set the dirty plates, glasses, and silverware on the left side of the sink. I wiped the bread crumbs off the right sink board, and I moved Iñaki's toaster oven, which we had not used.

There was a surprise underneath—two empty rifle shell casings. They were slender and less than an inch long—like small macaroni before it's been boiled. I picked them up and held them in my palm to show Justo.

He raised his eyebrows in surprise.

—Rifle, I said, knowing that Justo didn't like guns. He liked knives and hatchets and axes, and he had an assortment of sharp-bladed instruments from Spain.

"*No sé*," he said, shaking his head. I don't know.

I looked again at the brass casings, which looked like .22 magnum. They were rifle shells, bigger than the usual little .22 shells. I put them in my shirt pocket.

Justo's face lit up, and he smiled as if there was a good joke coming. —Now I remember, he said. He pointed at the kitchen window and past it. The house was on the edge of town, and the back yard looked out on farm land, barren now in the winter.

—My brother (Justo always said my brother, never Iñaki) used to kill jackrabbits in the garden.

177

—Did he eat jackrabbits? I looked at the toaster oven and imagined how the ejected casings must have rolled underneath.

—No, he killed them.

—Because they came in his garden?

—Oh, yeah, the ugly sonsofbitches.

I laughed, and Justo laughed. The .22 would have been a nice quiet gun for this kind of work at the edge of town. I imagined the bachelor Iñaki standing where I stood, cranking open the aluminum-framed kitchen window, and drygulching jackrabbits.

Before lunch, Justo and I had cleaned the rain gutters, raked leaves, straightened up the woodpile, and run the car engine for a while. After lunch, when the dishes were done, we went out front and picked a box of oranges to take home. It was a damp, overcast day, which was common at Christmas time, and the fruit was moist and cold. I asked if the dampness was bad for the oranges, and Justo said he would spread them out at home so they could dry off.

Justo and I speak Spanish with one another. It is my second language, and I get by all right with it. It is Justo's second language as well, Basque being his first and English being his third and weakest. When we had the box of oranges put away in his pickup, he asked if I would do him a favor and talk to the phone company.

I was glad to. Up until now I had been uncomfortable, to some extent, at puttering around this dead man's house and eating up his provisions. I knew Justo had taken the death pretty hard, and this was a way of making it manageable—a series of tasks. So we went inside to call the phone company.

In the dining room, underneath the bare light, stood a table with odds and ends of Iñaki's affairs—a bundle of cancelled checks, bills and envelopes, a 5 x 9 writing pad, a stick pen, a telephone book, and a pair of glasses. Justo sat down and pawed through the bills until he found what he needed. He put on his brother's glasses, read the notice, and pointed at it.

—They want us to call this number.

I looked at the letter and said yes. I said they wanted to know if they should continue service.

He said yes, but that the lawyer had told them not to pay any bills until they got the money straightened out. Justo's wife, who is American, had talked to the phone company, but someone needed to call again, to make sure they kept the service on.

I explained all of this to the service rep, who assured me that the account was in very good standing and had been so for many years. They just needed to know whether Mr. Echeverria's brother wanted to have service connected or disconnected.

The phone call helped me feel better. I sensed that Justo had invited me along so I could make the call, and so he would have someone around while he was tidying up his brother's affairs. I suppose also that he had wanted to have lunch, which was the kind of meal we had had for years, often just the two of us.

After the phone call, we went into the bathroom and tinkered with the toilet, so it would flush right. Justo had plans to rent out the house. I remarked that there wasn't much furniture, which there wasn't.

Except for a new-looking sofa that was covered with two fringed bedspreads, the house had very little. The dining room held the wooden table and three chairs, all old and worn. In the kitchen where we had eaten, stood a small table and two chairs, all wooden and painted white. The walls had few decorations, just a few small paintings and plaques showing Basque people in their native dress, feasting or working or dancing. These scenes are usually eight or ten inches square, and Justo's brother had an average of one per wall.

The bedroom was also spare. It had a narrow bed with a painted iron frame, a bureau with a mirror, and a tall upright chest of drawers. Over the head of the bed hung a crucifix, and the two side walls held the small plaques of Basque maidens, lads, and woodcutters.

Justo said that, no, there wasn't much furniture, that they would rent it as it was. He added that there had been a television set, a small new one, which he had taken home for safekeeping.

After the short tour of the house, Justo led me out through the kitchen and back porch, around to the side of the house, and into the basement. He used the English word "basement," even in Spanish. When we got there, it seemed more like a cellar. It was musty and dark, with light coming in through the small screened vents at ground level. Three of the concrete walls served as foundation for the house, while the fourth wall, the farthest from the steps leading in, ran only up to chin level. Beyond that, a dirt crawl space led back under the rest of the house.

Two hams, wrapped in cheesecloth, hung from a beam. Justo felt of them, pressed them between thumb and fingers, as I imagined he had done earlier when he fetched the one he had cut into for our lunch.

He nodded and then explained that he always hung his own hams here at his brother's, because a ventilated basement was best. And his house, of course, had no basement.

I nodded, felt the cool, firm hams, and took in their briny smell.

Next he moved a sheet of salvage plywood from in front of an open closet in a dark corner of the cellar. There, from chest to eye level, were three rows of wine bottles. I imagined the plywood served to keep out any light.

Below the wine bottles were two shelves of canned goods— jars of tomatoes on one shelf, and cloudy, dangerous-looking pickles on the other. Justo pulled out a bottle of wine here and there, inspected them, and chose two. He handed them to me and put the sheet of plywood back.

Justo took the two wine bottles from me, and, carrying them in what seemed to me a primitive way, in that darkened cellar, as if he were carrying two dead chickens, he headed towards the stairs. Then he stopped short and said, —Do you want to see the rifle?

I have a few guns myself, and I was interested in what it might look like. I said sure.

He set the two bottles on the floor and walked back to the wine closet. Setting the plywood aside again, he reached up inside the closet, to a shelf above the wine racks, and pulled out a rusty old carbine. It wasn't wrapped in a cloth or stuck in a scabbard or in any way taken care of.

He handed the gun to me. I hadn't seen one like it before. It was an old bolt action with a wooden stock, and it had two rings on it for a sling, I suppose, or for a saddle attachment. I looked at the barrel, which had a broad solid smear of rust and a thousand more specks. I couldn't find a caliber stamped on it, but it looked like an old .30 caliber of some kind.

—This isn't the gun he used for killing jackrabbits, I said.

—Is it a .30-30? he asked.

By the way he pronounced the numbers in Spanish, I knew he knew what one was. The .30-30 had always been a favorite coyote gun for sheepherders, and nine out of ten Basques I've known who came to this country started out herding sheep. Justo milked cows for a Portagee when he first came, but he knew a .30-30 by name even if he didn't know it by sight.

—I think so, I said. I slid the bolt open. The rifle had no shells in it. The magazine clip did not look long enough for .30-06 shells, but it looked about right for .30-30's. I pushed on the clip, and it fell out the underside of the gun, onto the floor. I picked up the clip and crammed it back in.

—I don't think this rifle has been any good for many years, I said.

—No?

—No, I don't think so. I don't think it's worth much.

I handed the gun to him, and he put it back up in the closet. He slid the plywood into its place, picked up the two bottles, and led the way out. At the door, he let me go ahead so he could lock up the basement.

I asked him if he wanted to take one of the hams, and he said he would take the one that was in the kitchen.

Upstairs, Justo set the wine bottles on the table by the reading glasses and the telephone, and he went in to use the bathroom. When he came out, I asked him if he thought the other rifle was still in the house.

He said he didn't know, but we could look.

I didn't like searching the dead man's house, so I watched Justo go through the hall closet, the bedroom closet, and then the big dresser, presumably just for good measure.

The only place left was the kitchen. I looked around at it as Justo peeked into the broom closet and under the sink. All of the cabinets, like the door leading to the back porch, had been painted white a long time ago. By the door handle, by the handle of each cabinet door, as well as by the refrigerator door handle and on the backs of the two chairs, smudges had accumulated from years of contact with unwashed hands. I had noticed a general uncleanliness earlier, but now I saw how uniform it was.

After his thorough rummaging, Justo looked at me and shook his head. Then we both scanned the cupboards and walls. I think we saw it at the same time—a hatch lid above the sink. We looked at each other with raising eyebrows. Justo pulled over one of the two chairs and motioned for me to go ahead.

I stepped onto the chair and then onto the sink board, straddling the single sink. The hatch lid was masonite and pushed up easily. I rotated it, slid it out, and held it in my left hand. Then I reached up and into the ceiling with my right hand, as I now imagine Iñaki must have done, and I laid my hand on the smooth cool stock of a rifle.

I moved my hand up the stock and felt that it was a lever action. I closed my hand around the narrow part of the stock and lifted the rifle up, out, and down into the kitchen.

It was a Winchester .22 magnum, not a cheap model. The gun was sleek and pretty, with a polished stock and forearm and a glistening blue-black barrel.

—What do you think? I said.

Justo nodded.

—Shall we take it with us?

He looked uncertain. —Put it back up there, he said, and I'll get it some other time.

I put the gun away, set the lid back in the hatch, and jumped down.

On the way back to Sacramento, I asked Justo why his brother would put such a pretty rifle in a place like that.

He said his brother probably kept it in with the broom, so he could take it out right away when a jackrabbit showed up, and he probably hid it when he went to the hospital.

I asked him if his brother was in the habit of hiding money in the house.

Oh, no, he said. His brother had saved over two hundred thousand dollars in the twenty-seven years he'd been here, and he had it all in the bank. He had always been afraid the house would burn down.

—Why did he leave the rifle there, then? I asked.

"*¿Quién sabe?*" he said. Who knows?

* * * * *

That evening, while Justo was taking a bath, I sat by the fire and told his wife, Carol, about the rifle.

"Iñaki was a very private man," she said.

"I barely knew him," I said. "I think I met him only once, several years ago."

"He was very private. He rarely went anywhere to enjoy himself. He avoided women. I don't think he liked them. But even some of his men friends found him to be strange. Sometimes he would hide in the house and not answer the door, and yet they knew he was there."

"That does sound strange. And sad."

"Yes, and you know, for several years at Christmas, I would give him a shirt or a sweater, and when he passed away, they were all still in their packages, stacked in the closet. He never even unfolded them." She blew her nose and said, "He meant a lot to Justo. It really hurt him when his brother died."

When Justo was done with his bath, he poured us his favorite highball, whiskey and Seven-Up, which he called Seven High. Our talk was all about the weather, the Forty-Niners, how long I was going to stay, when I would visit again, and why we should go to Spain some time.

That night I slept in a big bed with clean sheets, warm blankets, and a soft pillow. Before I went to sleep, I remembered stories I had heard—or more accurately, I remembered images from stories I had heard. One was of a machine shop on an aircraft carrier, a large room that had been sheeted and riveted over, until one day someone figured it out from a floor plan and opened up the room. It was fully equipped and furnished with new lathes, drills, and presses. Another image was of a house, a large house, where a similar mistake had caused an empty bedroom to be paneled off for decades. And yet another was about a room in an old stone mansion, a room that had been occupied and furnished and then masoned off, sealed, for no reason apparent to the heirs.

I remember thinking of those stories, and I remember that just before I fell asleep, I wondered what he did with the jackrabbits.

About the Author

John D. Nesbitt lives in the plains country of Wyoming, where he teaches English and Spanish at Eastern Wyoming College. His articles, reviews, fiction, and poetry have appeared in numerous magazines and anthologies. He has had more than thirty books published, including short story collections, contemporary novels, and traditional westerns, as well as textbooks for his courses. John has won many awards for his work, including two awards from the Wyoming State Historical Society (for fiction), two awards from Wyoming Writers for encouragement of other writers and service to the organization, two Wyoming Arts Council literary fellowships (one for fiction, one for non-fiction), a Will Rogers Medallion Award for *Dark Prairie* (a frontier mystery) and another for *Thorns on the Rose* (a poetry collection), a Western Writers of America Spur finalist award for his novel *Raven Springs*, and the Spur award itself for his short story "At the End of the Orchard" and for his novels *Trouble at the Redstone* and *Stranger in Thunder Basin*. His recent work includes *Poacher's Moon,* a contemporary novel; *Blue Horse Mesa*, a collection of western stories; and *Field Work*, a retro-noir fiction collection. Visit his website at www.johndnesbitt.com

"NESBITT IS A
TRUE ARTIST."
—WESTERN
AMERICAN
LITERATURE

John D. Nesbitt
TWO NOVELLAS

Published by SpeakingVolumes

Visit us at www.speakingvolumes.us

John D. Nesbitt

NOT A RUSTLER

"NESBITT IS A TRUE ARTIST."
—WESTERN AMERICAN LITERATURE

Published by SpeakingVolumes

Visit us at www.speakingvolumes.us

Visit us at www.speakingvolumes.us

John D. Nesbitt

MAN FROM
WOLF RIVER

"NESBITT IS A TRUE ARTIST."
—WESTERN AMERICAN LITERATURE

Published by SpeakingVolumes

Visit us at www.speakingvolumes.us

Visit us at